# BENNY AND PENNY

*IN*

# THE BIG NO-NO!

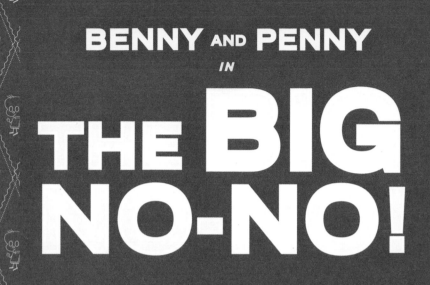

# GEOFFREY HAYES

# BENNY AND PENNY

*IN*

# THE BIG NO-NO!

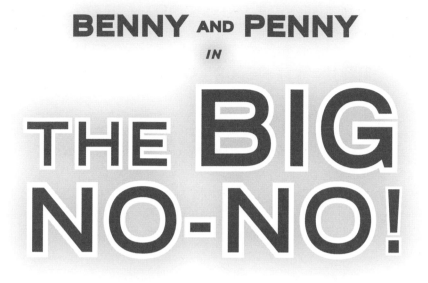

A TOON BOOK BY

# GEOFFREY HAYES

TOON BOOKS IS A DIVISION OF RAW JUNIOR, LLC, NEW YORK

# THE 2010 THEODOR SEUSS GEISEL AWARD WINNER

given annually by the ALA's Association for Library Service to Children to the author of
"the most distinguished American book for beginning readers published in the United States."

## KIRKUS BEST OF '09 CONTINUING SERIES

# For Debby Carter

Editorial Director: FRANÇOISE MOULY

Book Design: FRANÇOISE MOULY & JONATHAN BENNETT

GEOFFREY HAYES' artwork was drawn in colored pencil.

Library of Congress Cataloging-in-Publication Data:

Hayes, Geoffrey.

  Benny and Penny in The big no-no! : a Toon Book / by Geoffrey Hayes.

     p. cm.

  Summary: Two mice meet their new neighbor and discover that she is not as scary as they feared.

  ISBN 978-0-9799238-9-0

  1. Graphic novels. [1. Graphic novels. 2. Mice–Fiction. 3. Brothers and sisters–Fiction. 4. Neighbors–Fiction.]

  I. Title. II. Title: Big no-no!

  PZ7.7.H39Be 2009

  [E]–dc22

                    2008036307

          ISBN 13: 978-0-9799238-9-0  ISBN 10: 0-9799238-9-1

                10 9 8 7 6 5 4 3 2

www.TOON-BOOKS.com

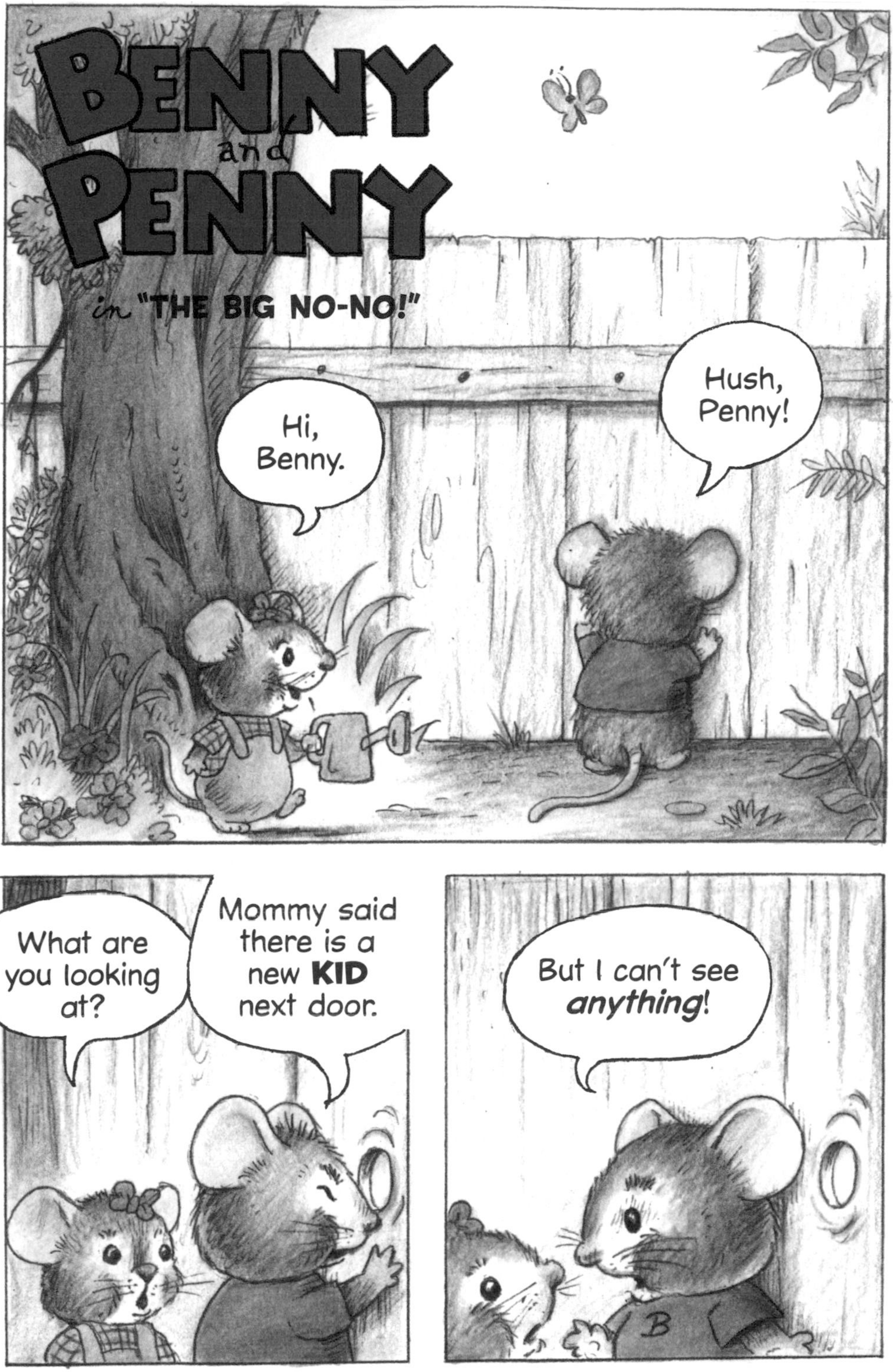
BENNY and PENNY
in "THE BIG NO-NO!"
Hi, Benny.
Hush, Penny!
What are you looking at?
Mommy said there is a new **KID** next door.
But I can't see ***anything***!

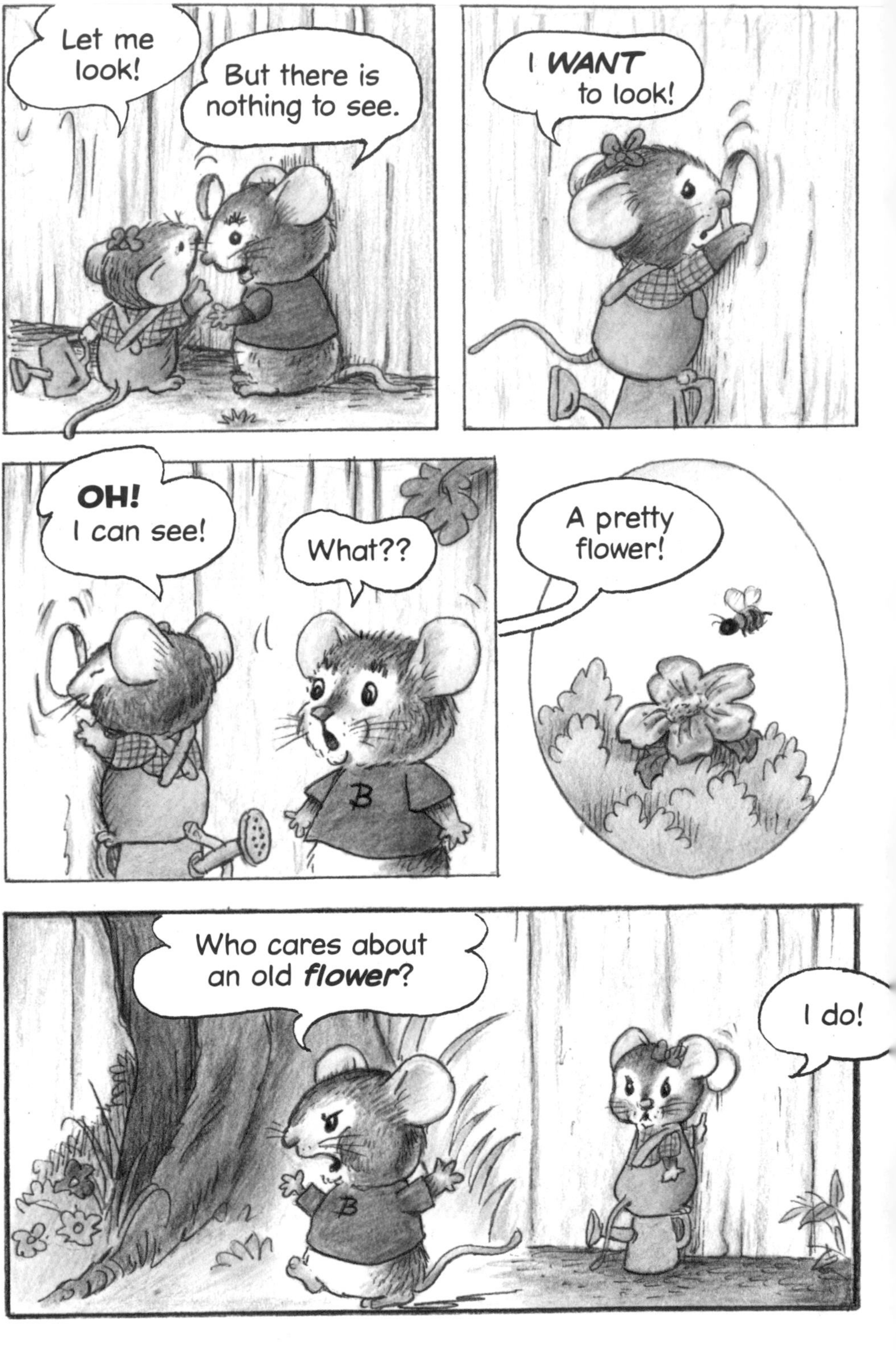
Let me look!
But there is nothing to see.
I WANT to look!
OH! I can see!
What??
A pretty flower!
Who cares about an old flower?
I do!

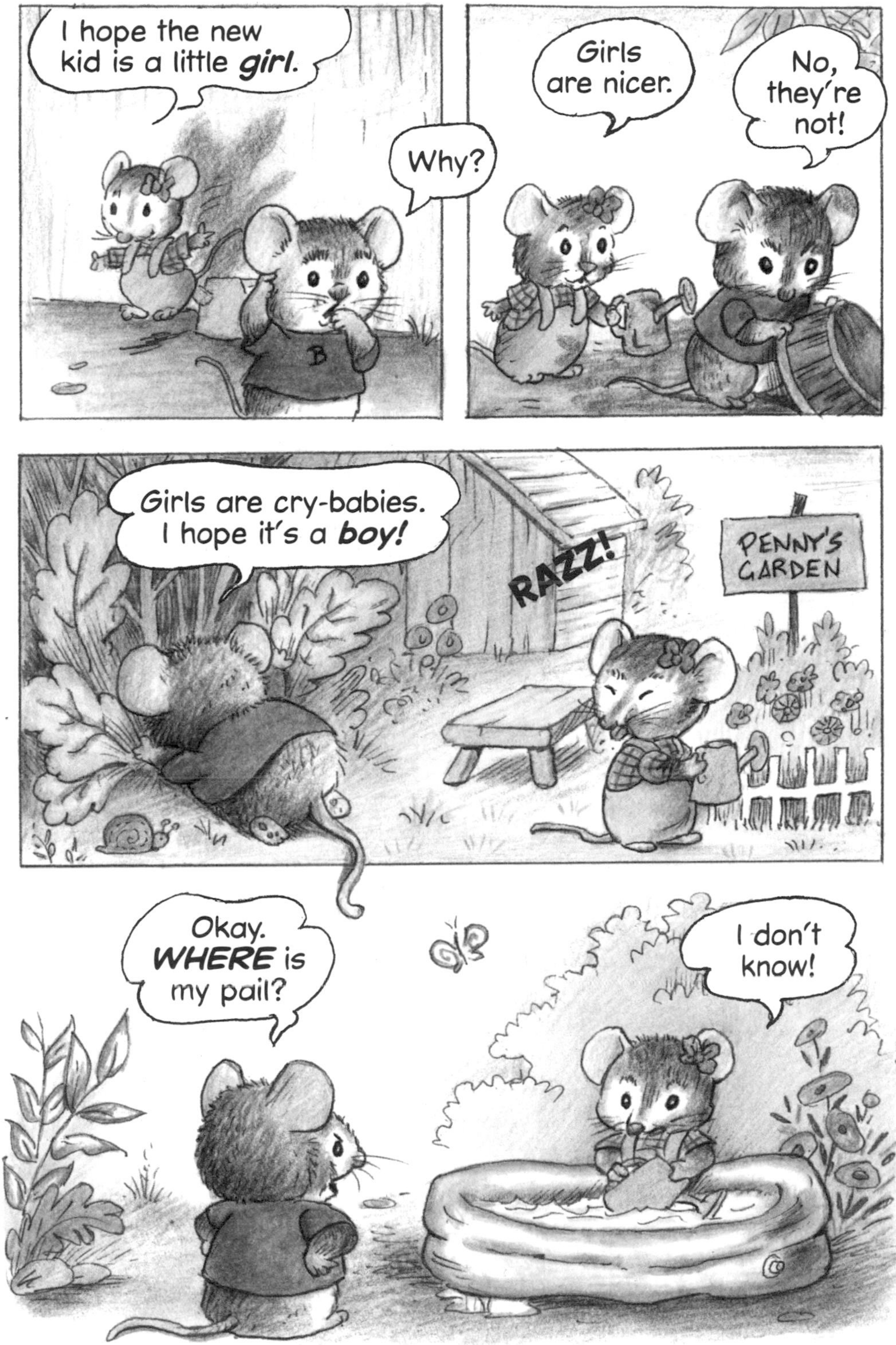
I hope the new kid is a little *girl*.
Why?
Girls are nicer.
No, they're not!
Girls are cry-babies. I hope it's a *boy!*
RAZZ!
PENNY'S GARDEN
Okay. *WHERE* is my pail?
I don't know!

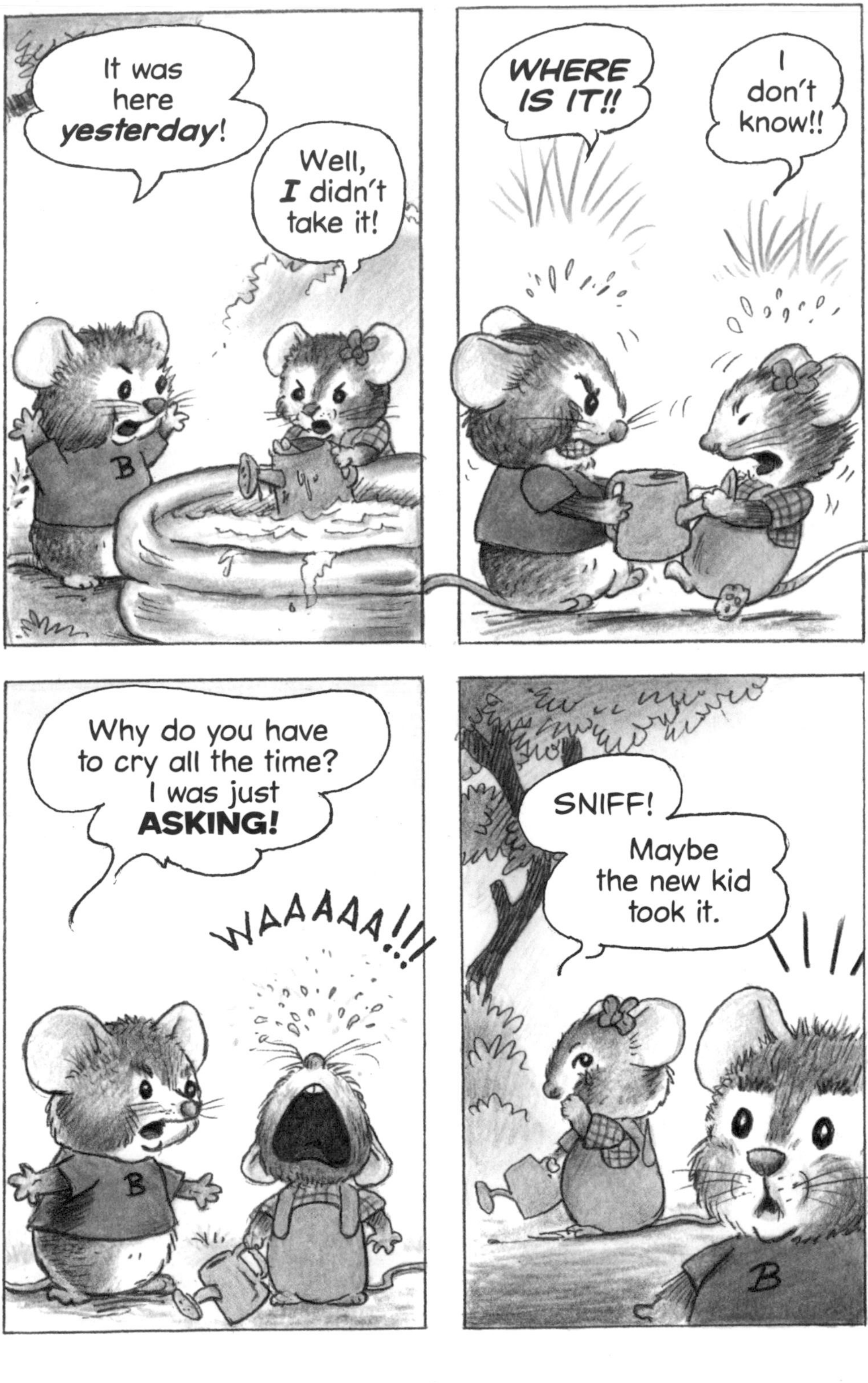
It was here yesterday!
Well, I didn't take it!
WHERE IS IT!!
I don't know!!
Why do you have to cry all the time? I was just ASKING!
WAAAAA!!!
SNIFF!
Maybe the new kid took it.

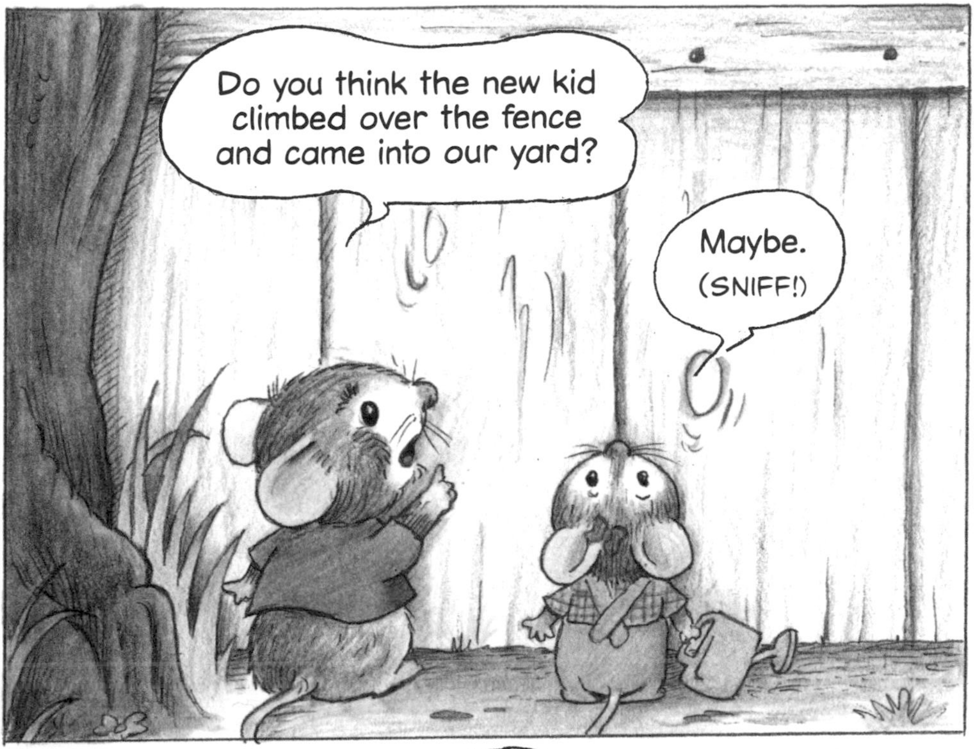
Do you think the new kid climbed over the fence and came into our yard?
Maybe. (SNIFF!)

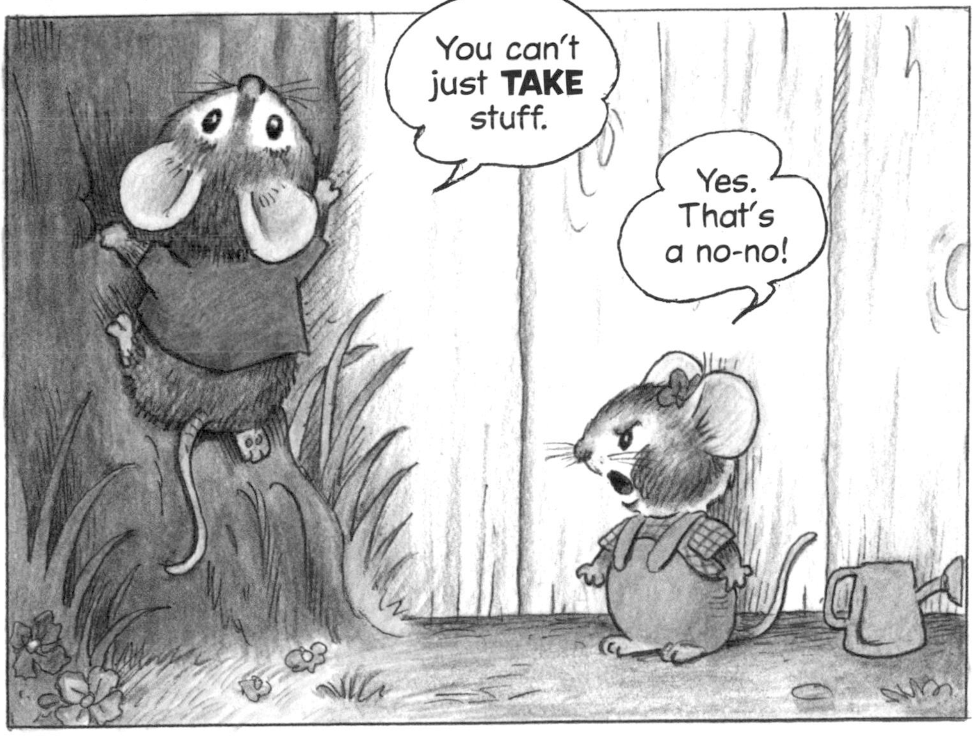
You can't just **TAKE** stuff.
Yes. That's a no-no!

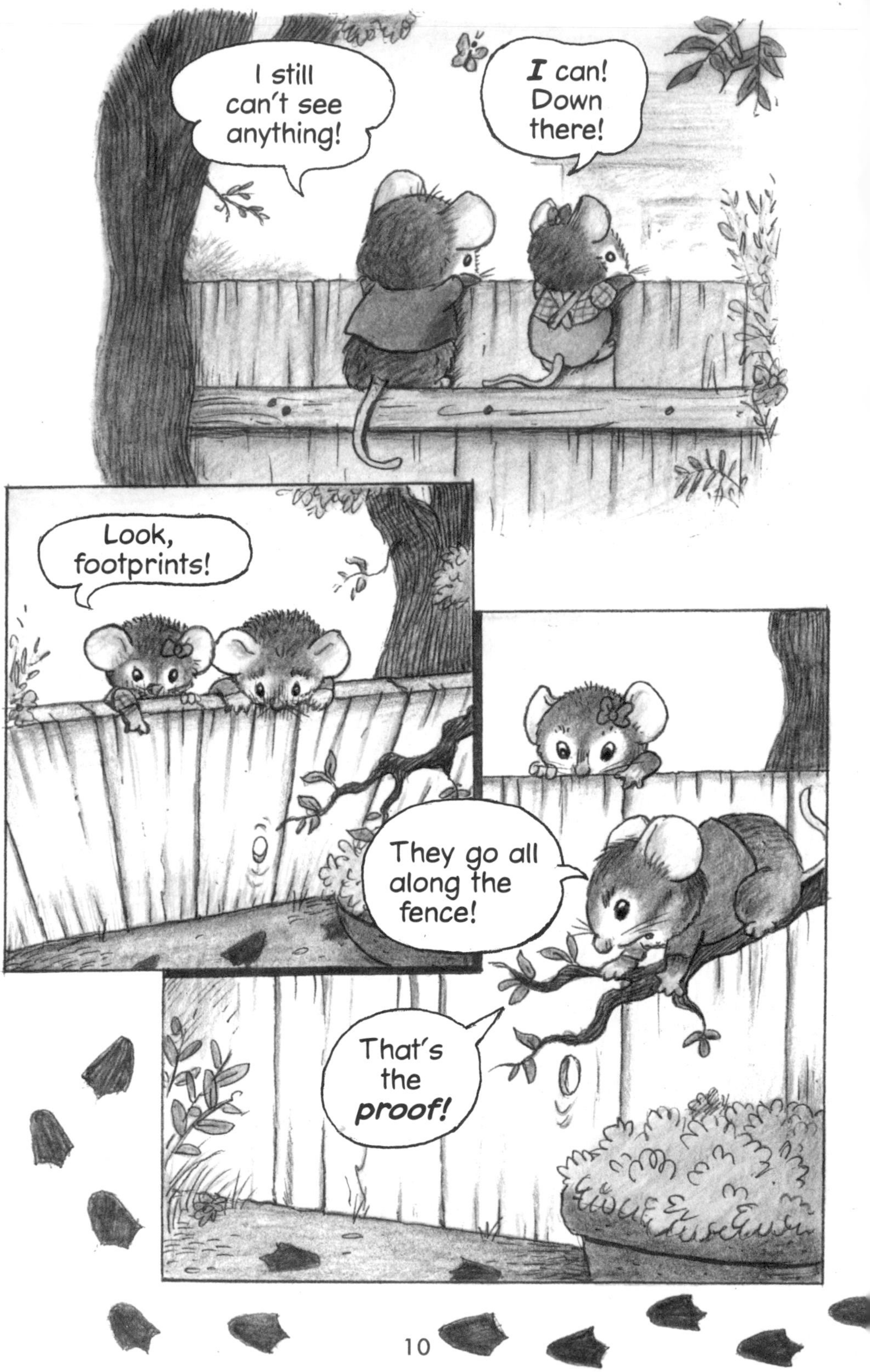
I still can't see anything!
*I* can! Down there!
Look, footprints!
They go all along the fence!
That's the ***proof!***

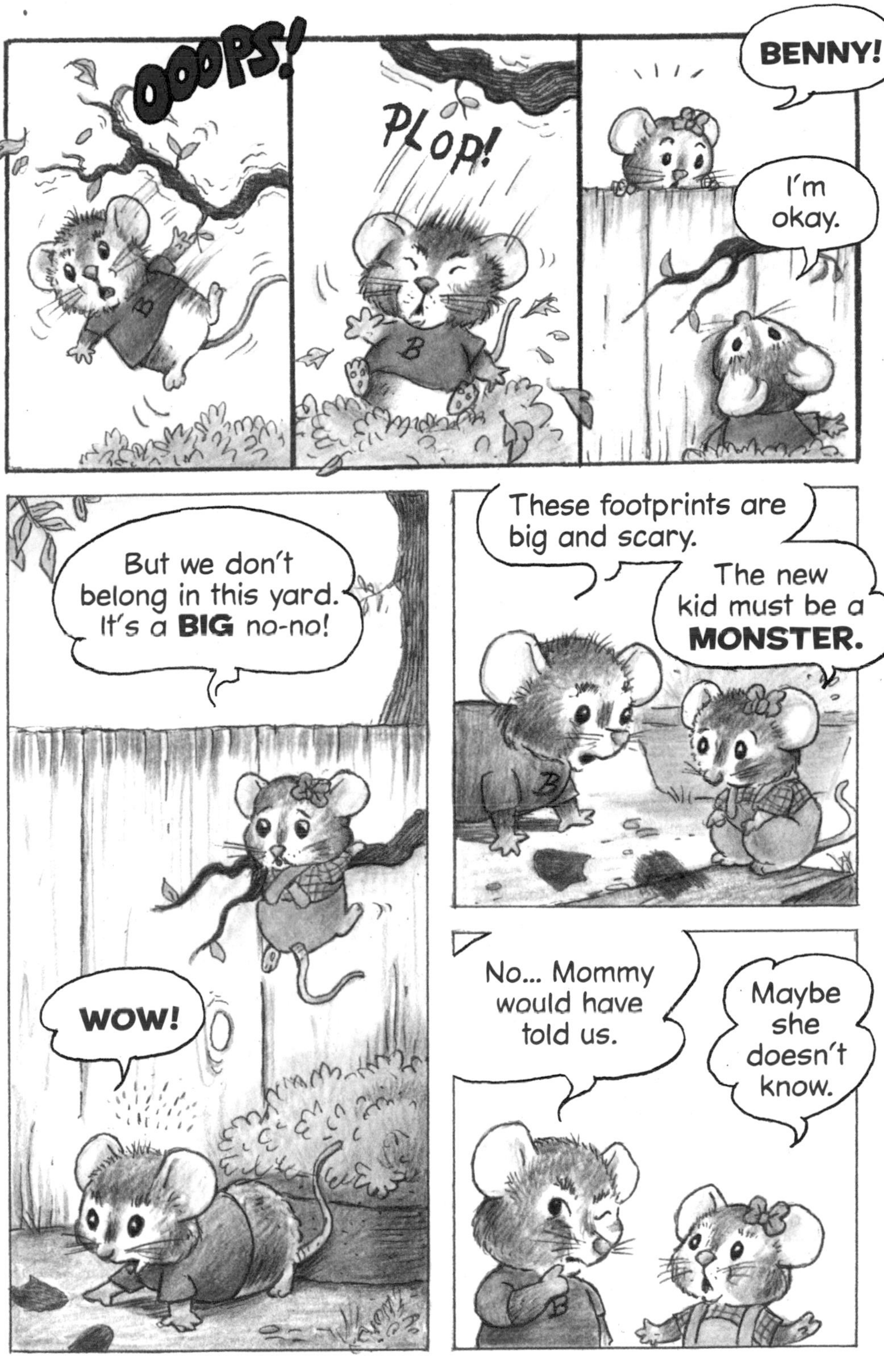
OOOPS!
PLOP!
BENNY!
I'm okay.
But we don't belong in this yard. It's a **BIG** no-no!
WOW!
These footprints are big and scary.
The new kid must be a **MONSTER.**
No... Mommy would have told us.
Maybe she doesn't know.

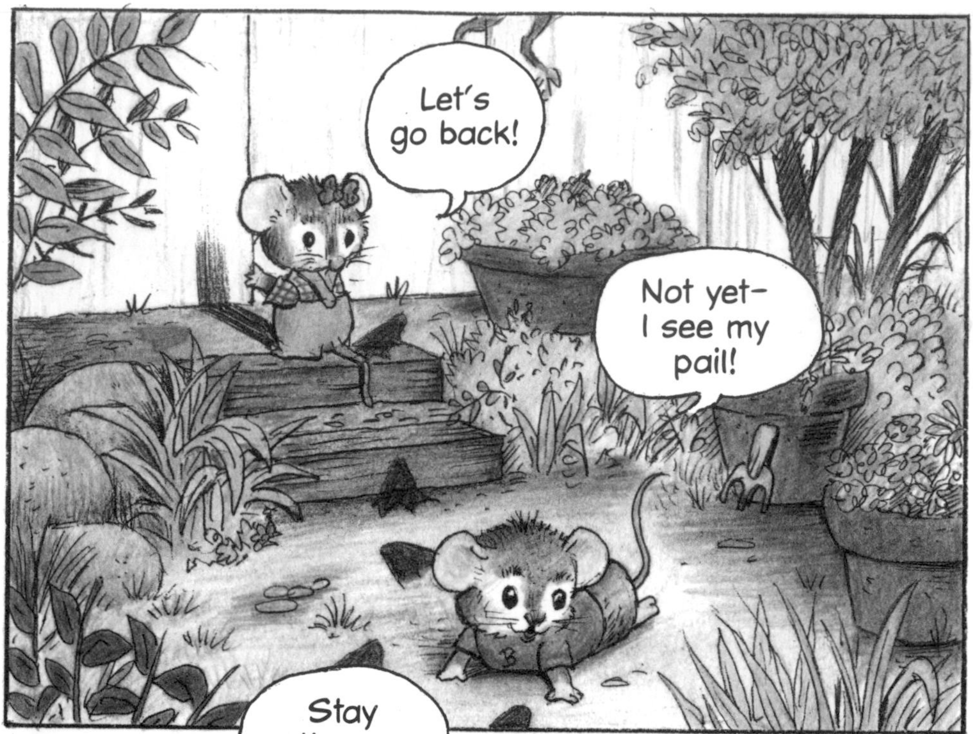
Let's go back!
Not yet- I see my pail!

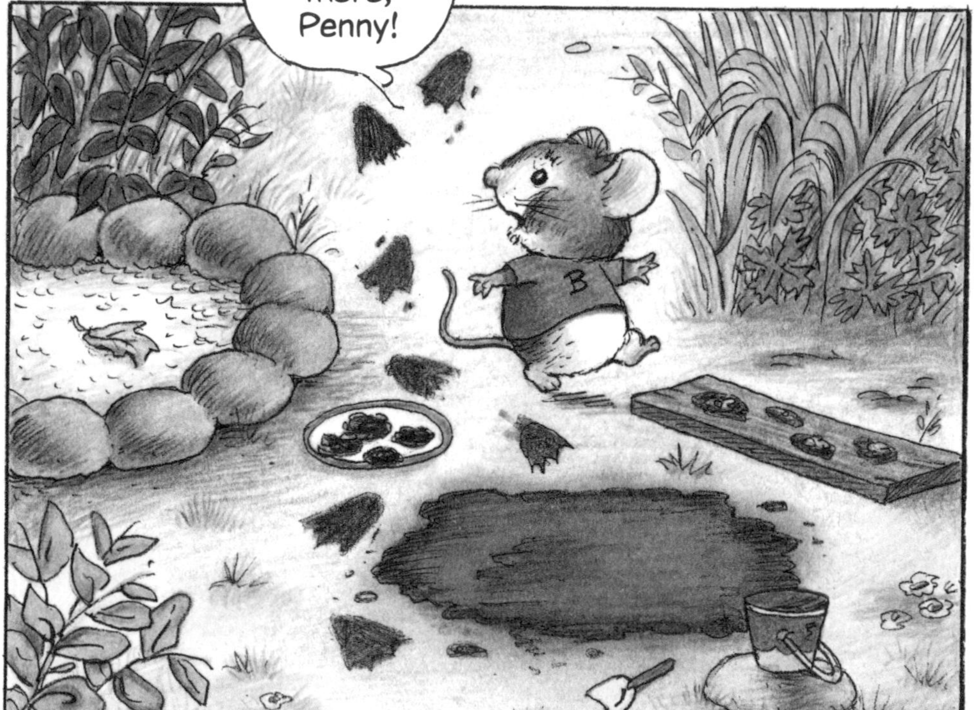
Stay there, Penny!

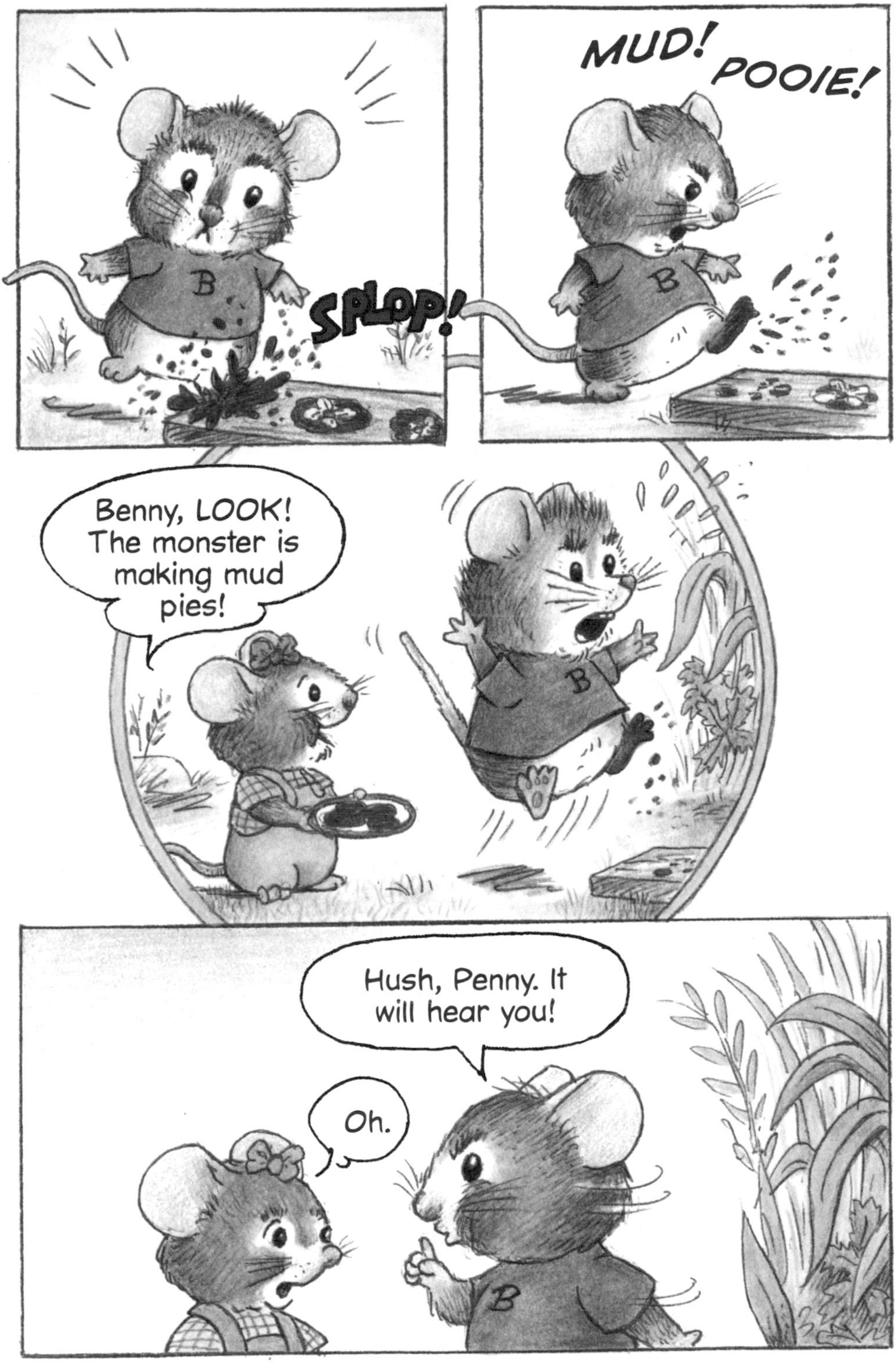
SPLOP!
MUD! POOIE!
Benny, LOOK! The monster is making mud pies!
Hush, Penny. It will hear you!
Oh.

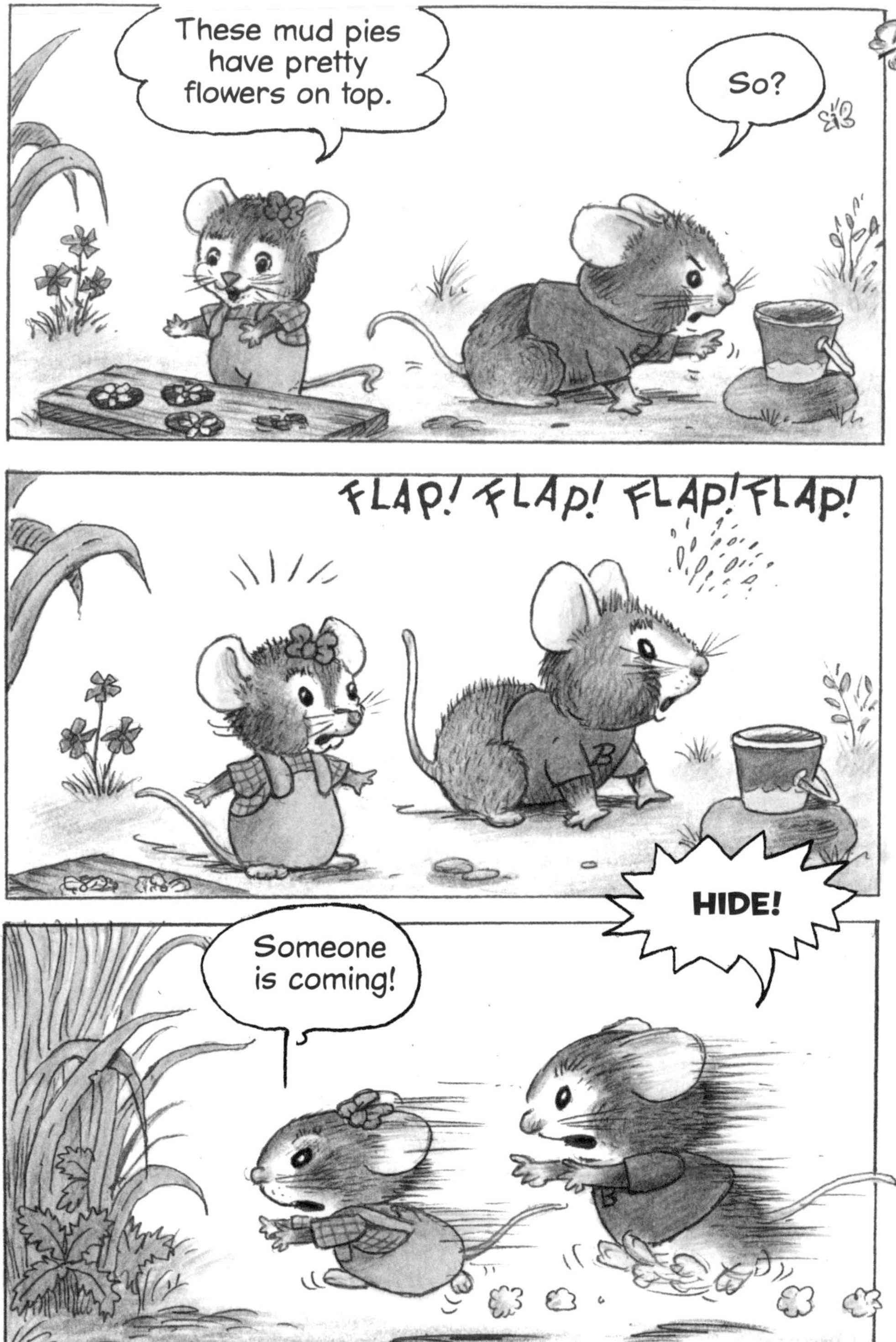
These mud pies have pretty flowers on top.
So?
FLAP! FLAP! FLAP! FLAP!
HIDE!
Someone is coming!

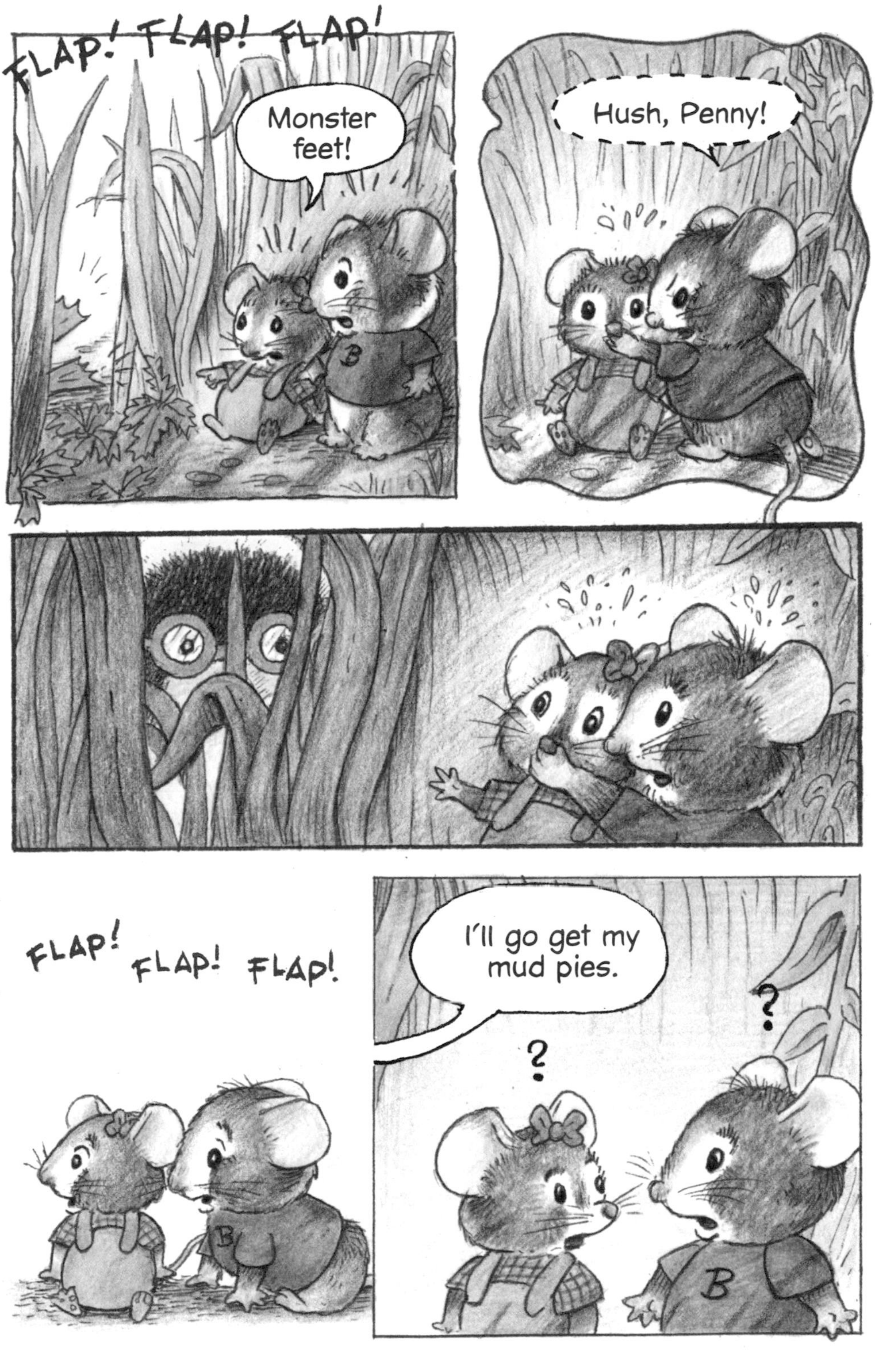
FLAP! FLAP! FLAP!
Monster feet!
Hush, Penny!
FLAP! FLAP! FLAP!
I'll go get my mud pies.
?
?

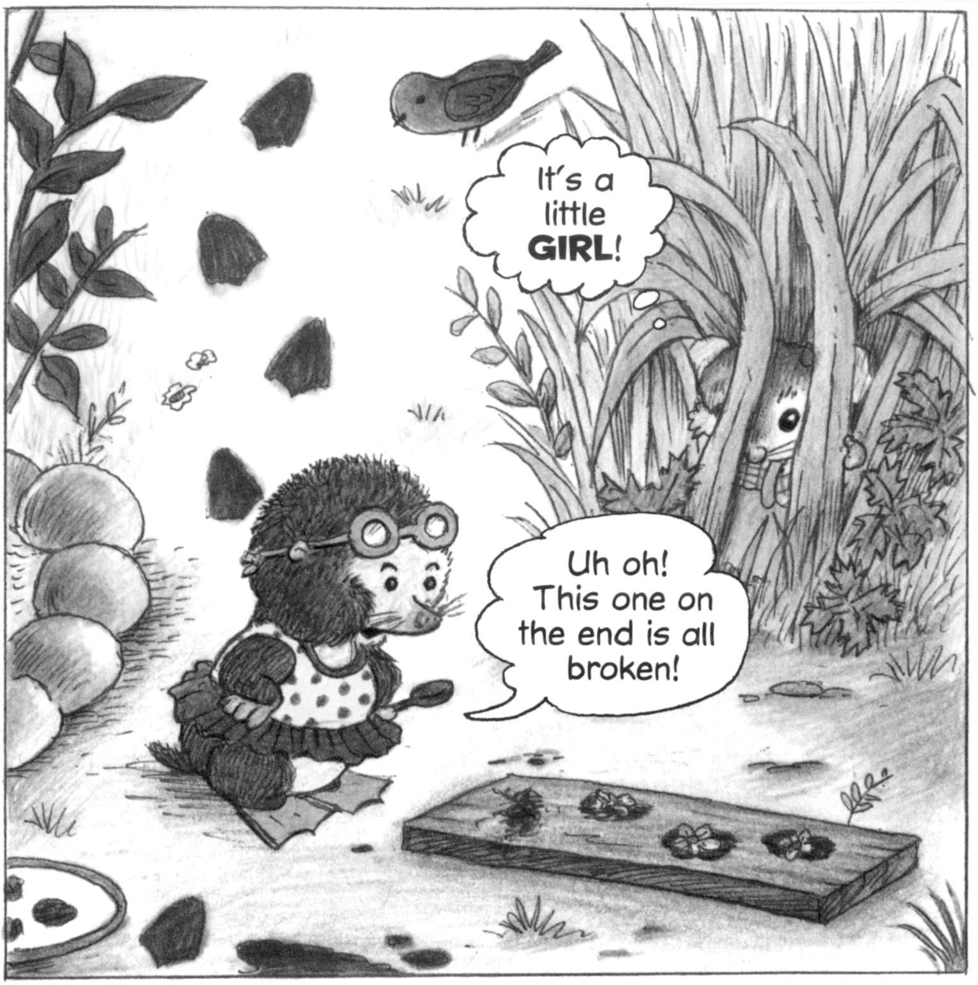
It's a little **GIRL**!
Uh oh! This one on the end is all broken!

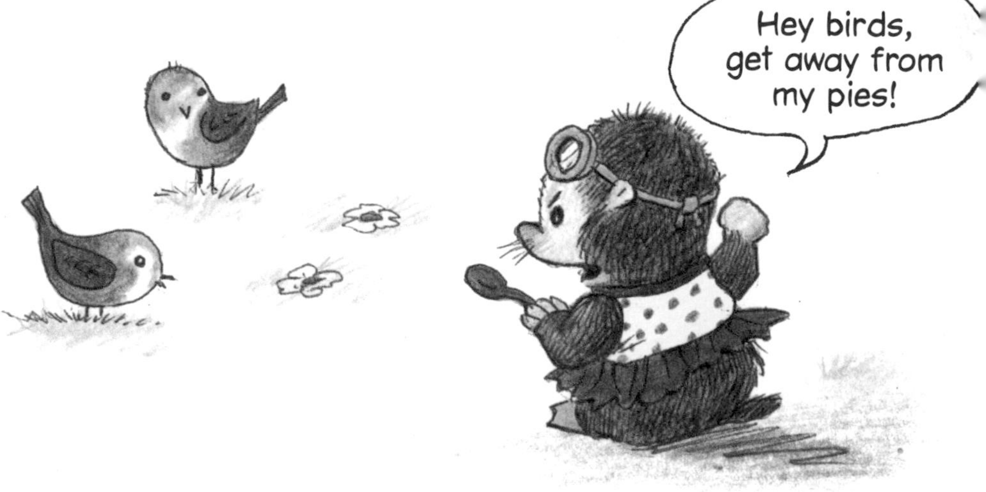
Hey birds, get away from my pies!

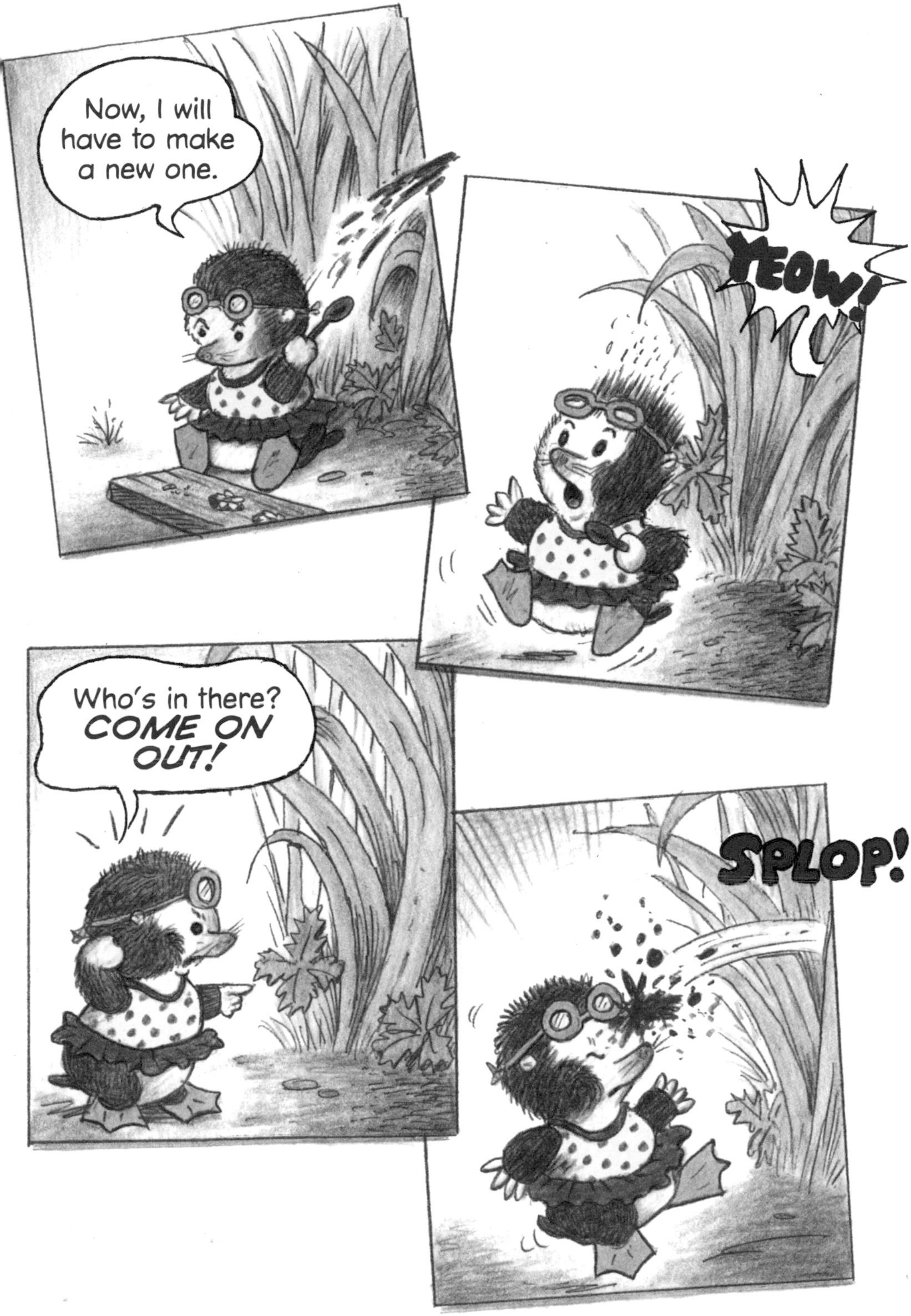
Now, I will have to make a new one.
YEOW!
Who's in there? COME ON OUT!
SPLOP!

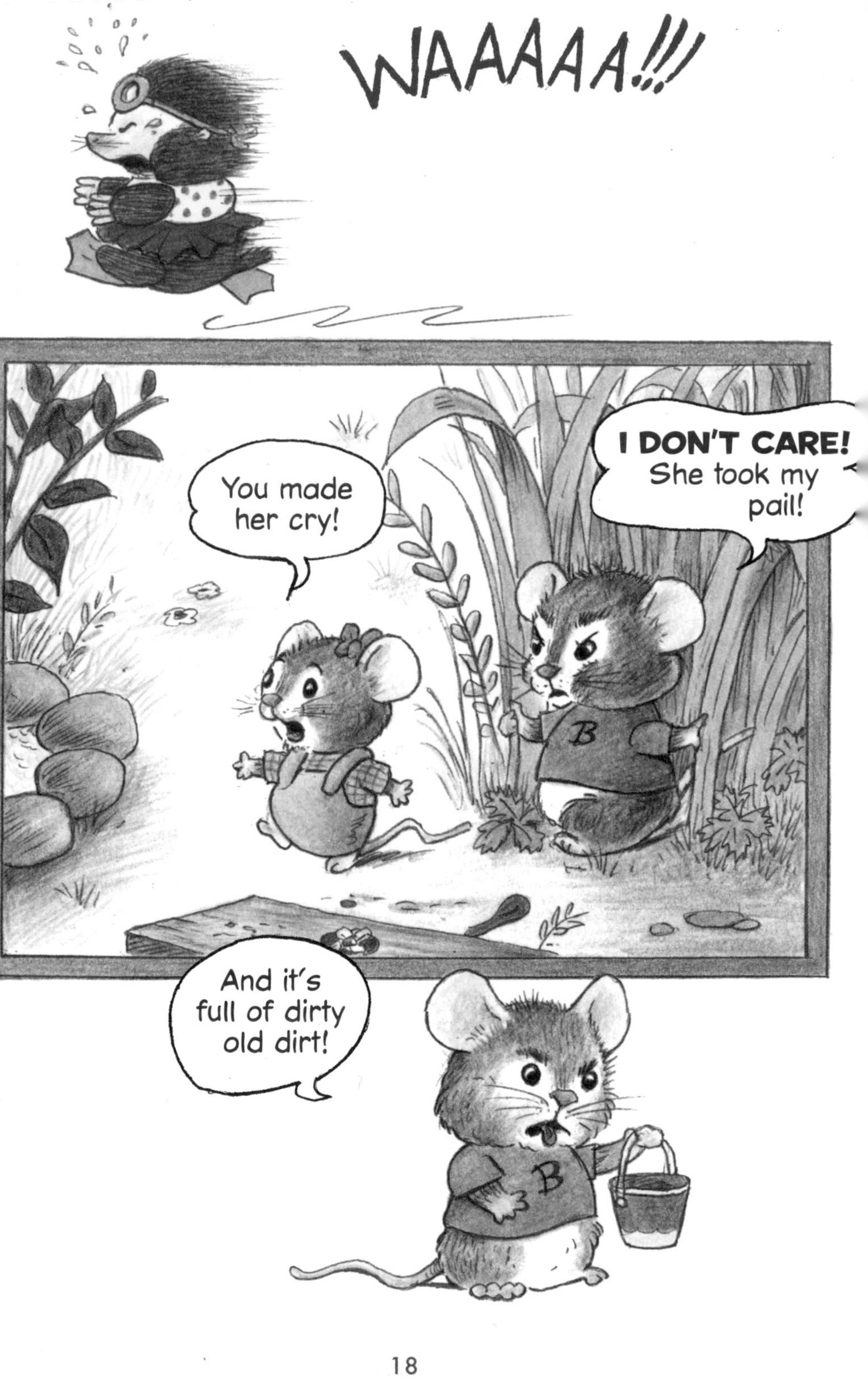
WAAAAA!!!
You made her cry!
I DON'T CARE! She took my pail!
And it's full of dirty old dirt!

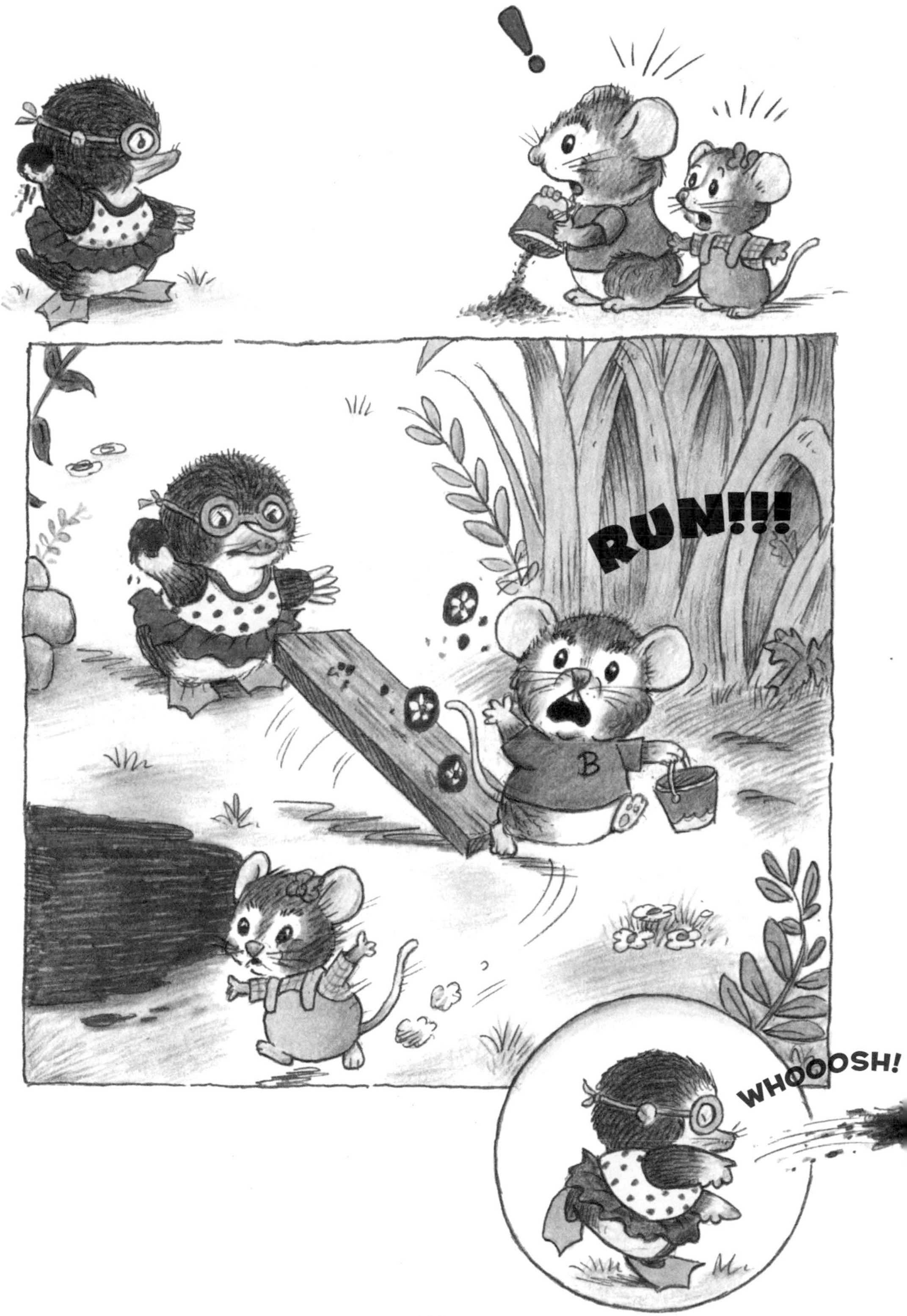
RUN!!!
WHOOOSH!

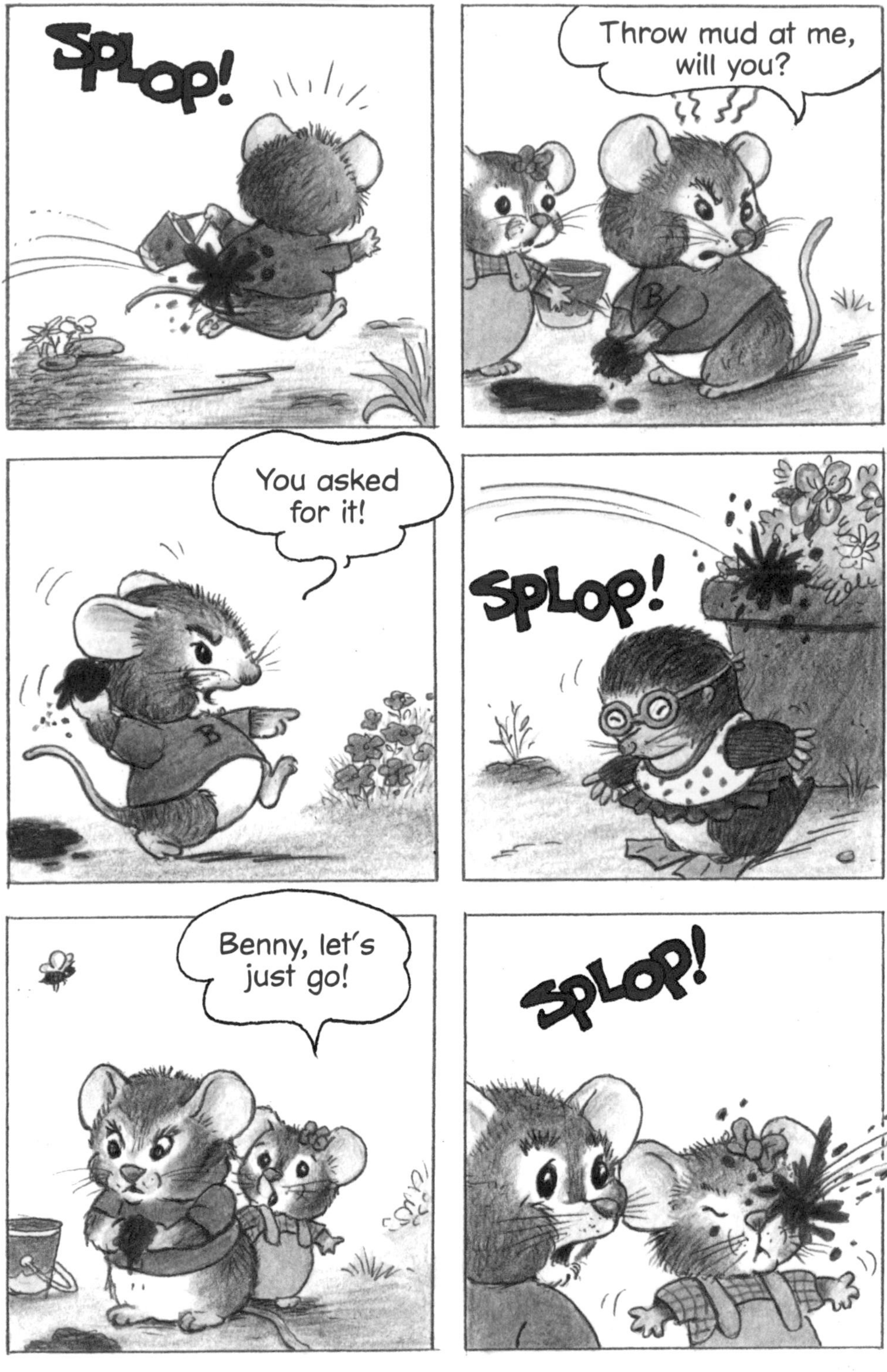
SPLOP!
Throw mud at me, will you?
You asked for it!
SPLOP!
Benny, let's just go!
SPLOP!

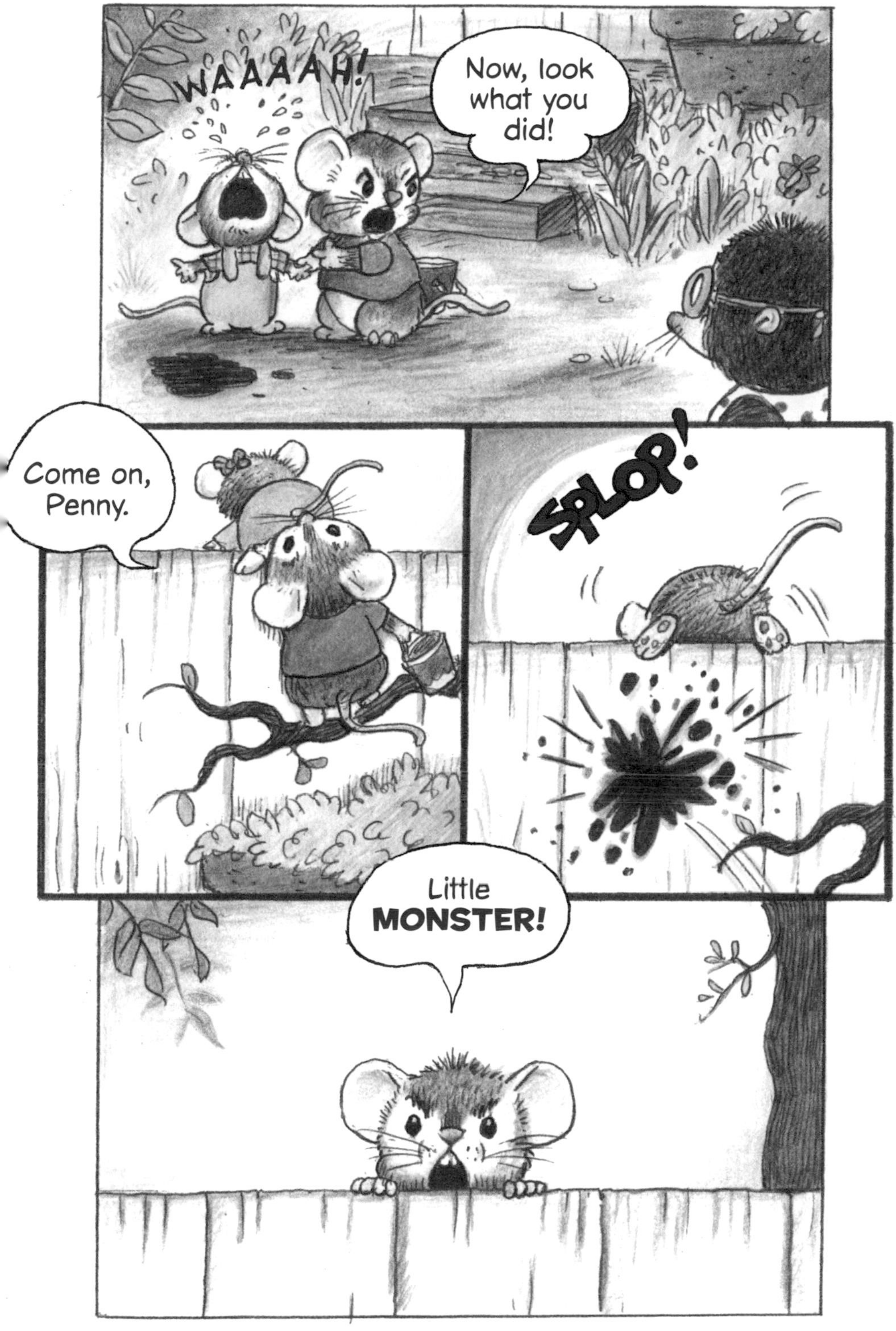
WAAAAH!
Now, look what you did!
Come on, Penny.
SPLOP!
Little MONSTER!

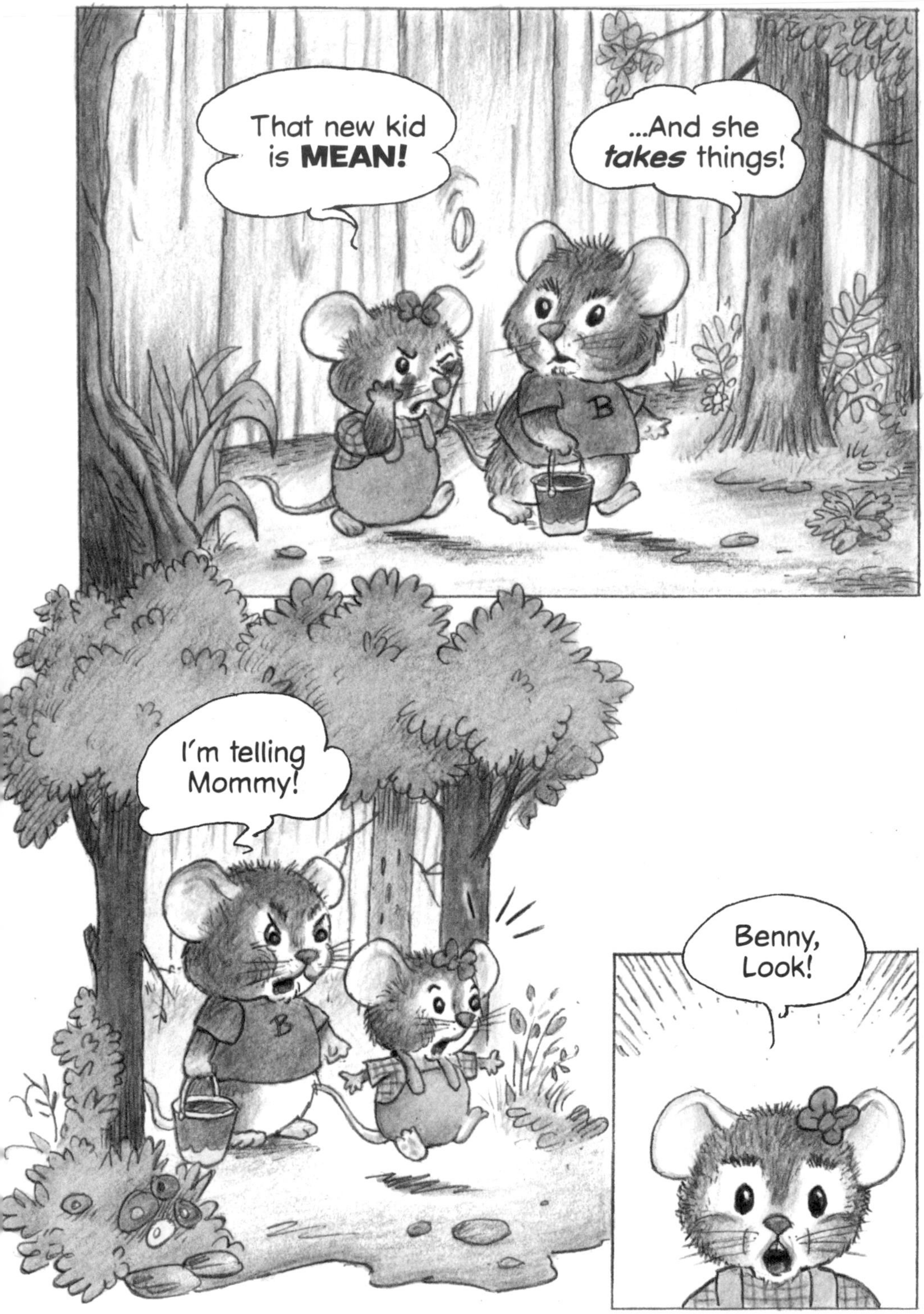
That new kid is **MEAN!**
...And she *takes* things!
I'm telling Mommy!
Benny, Look!

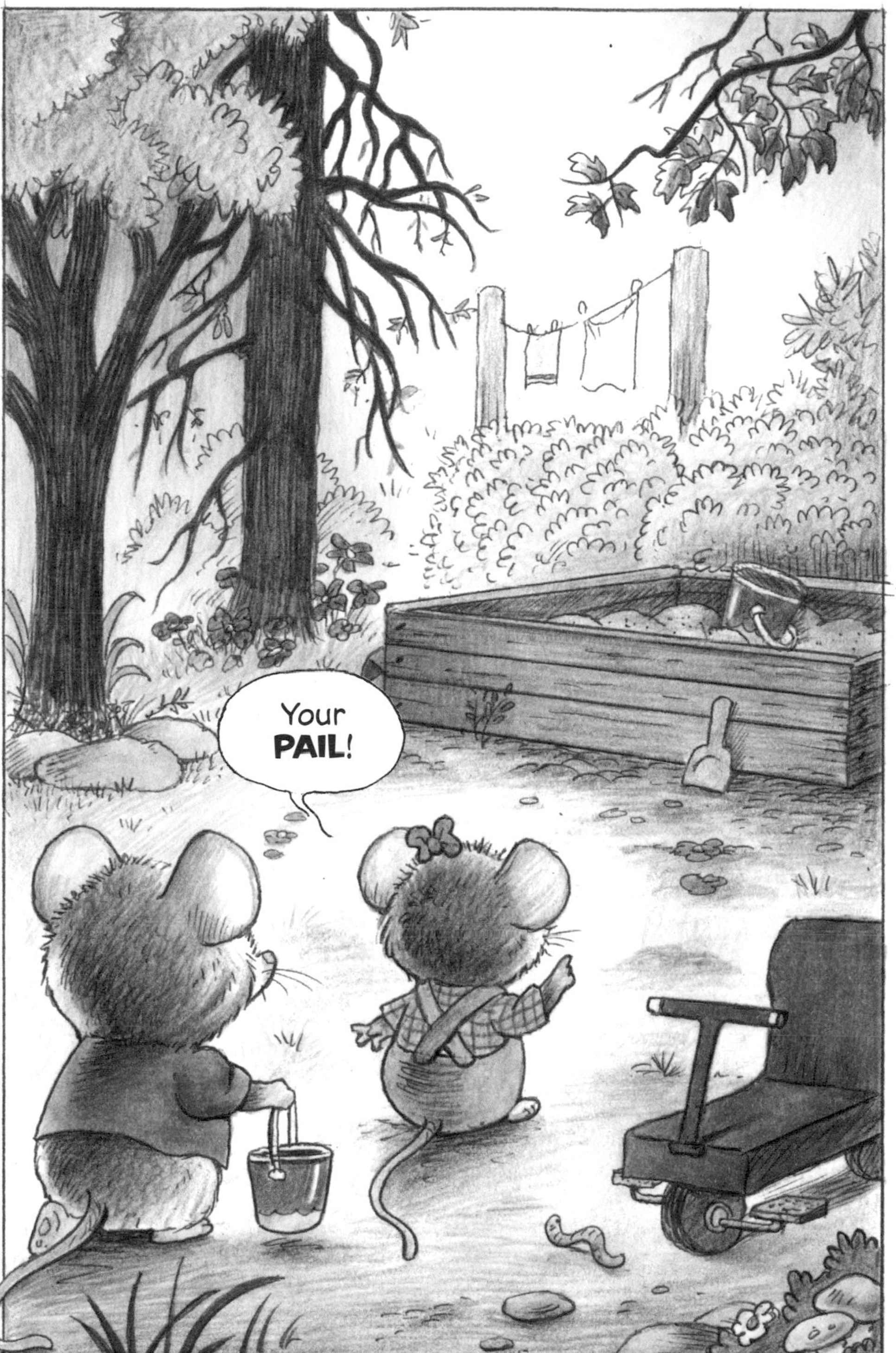
Your **PAIL**!

24

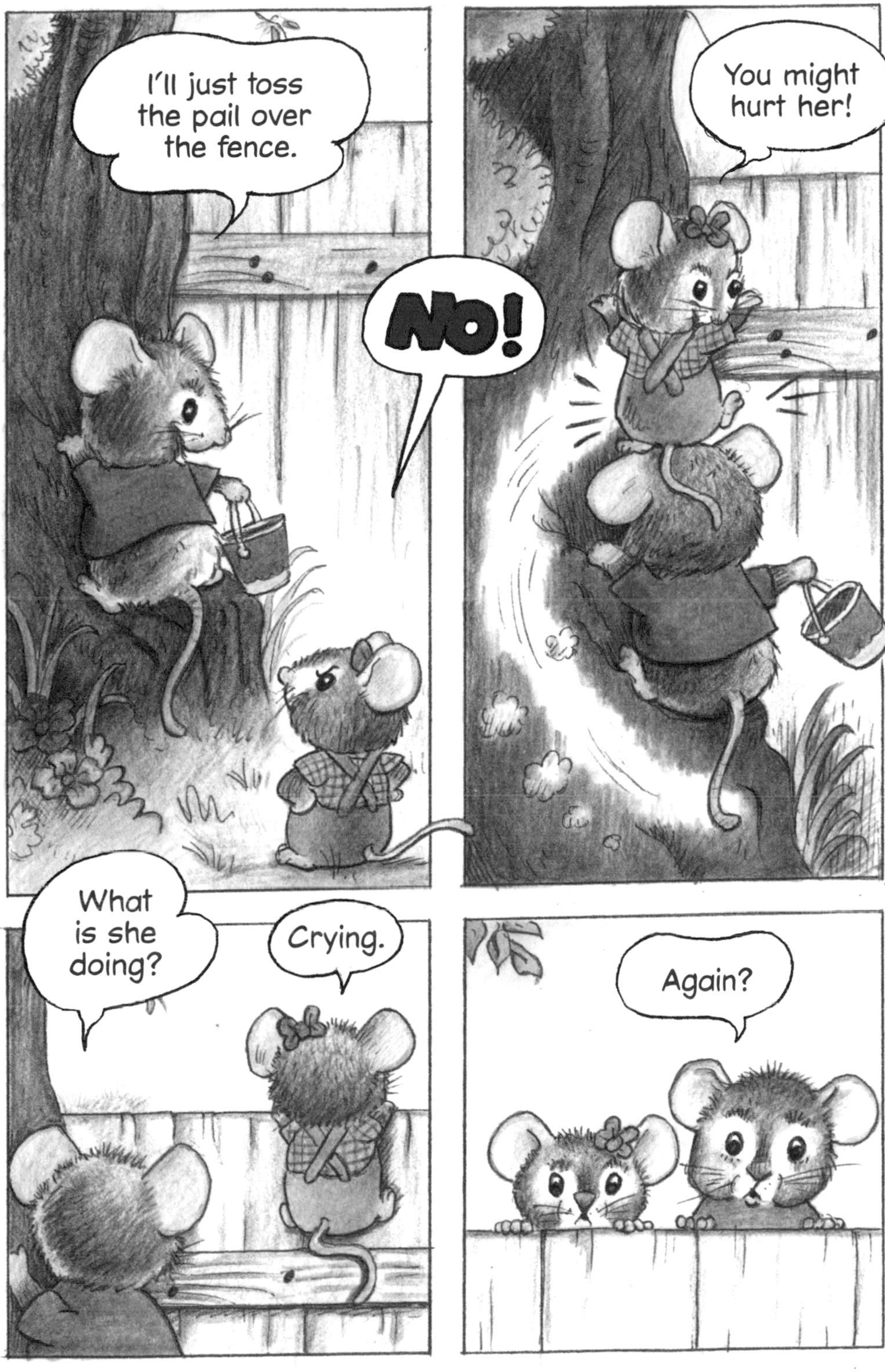
I'll just toss the pail over the fence.
NO!
You might hurt her!
What is she doing?
Crying.
Again?

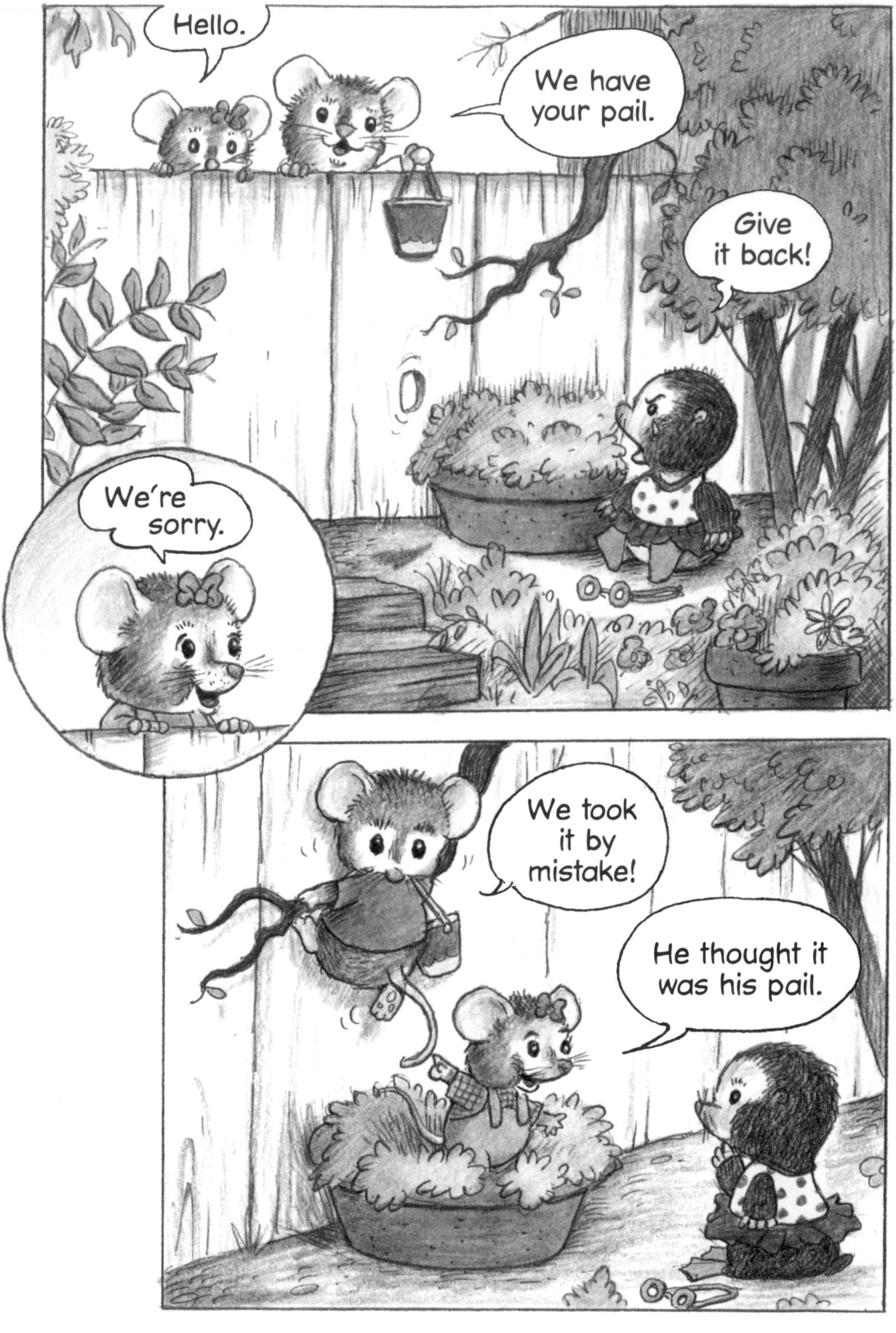
Hello.
We have your pail.
Give it back!
We're sorry.
We took it by mistake!
He thought it was his pail.

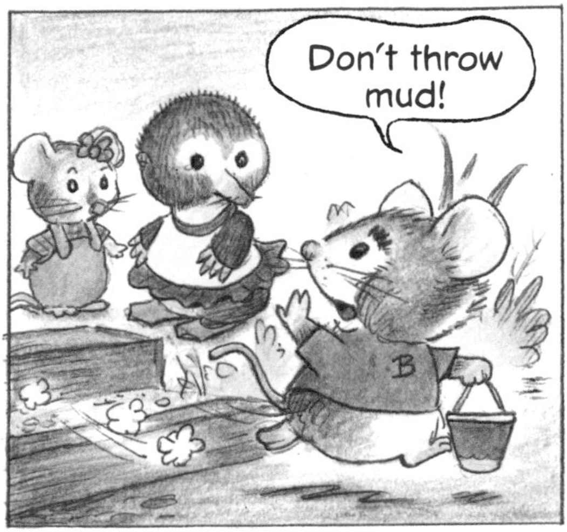
Don't throw mud!

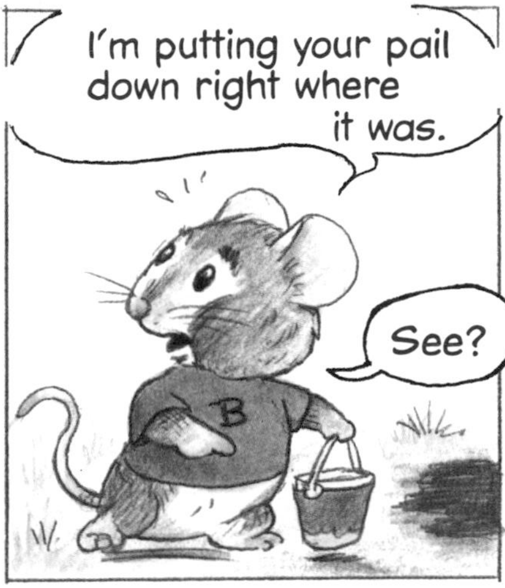
I'm putting your pail down right where it was.
See?

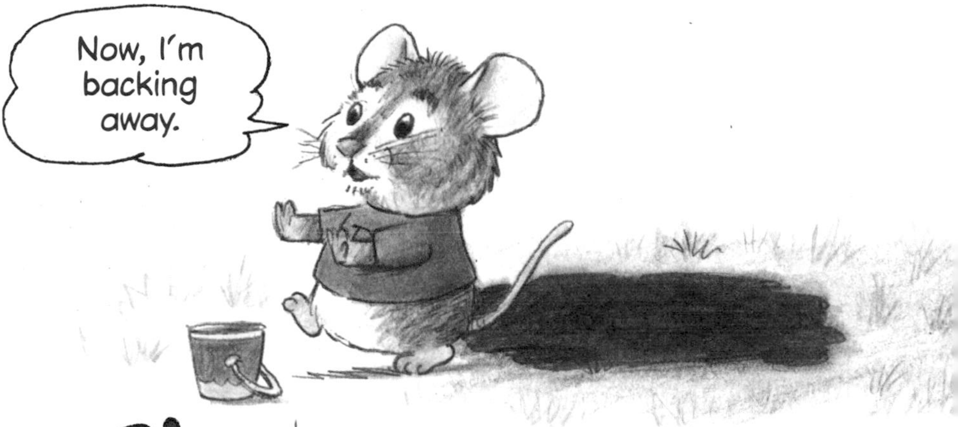
Now, I'm backing away.

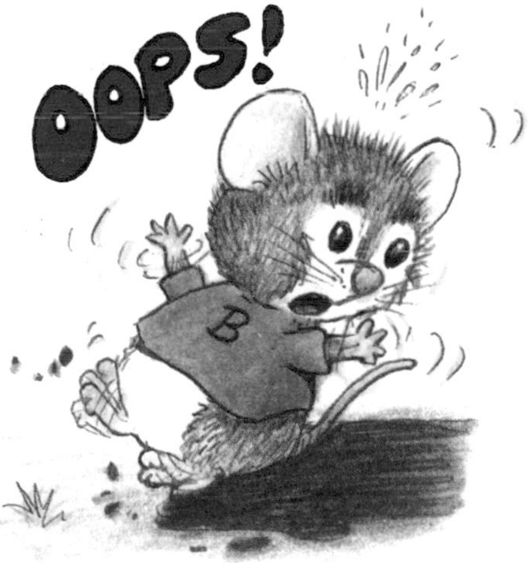
OOPS!

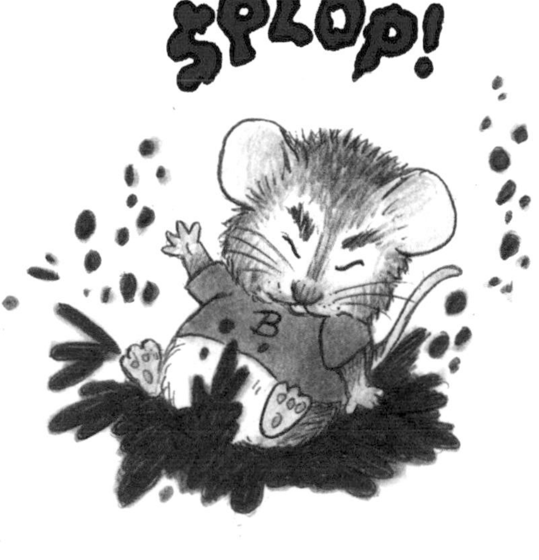
SPLOP!

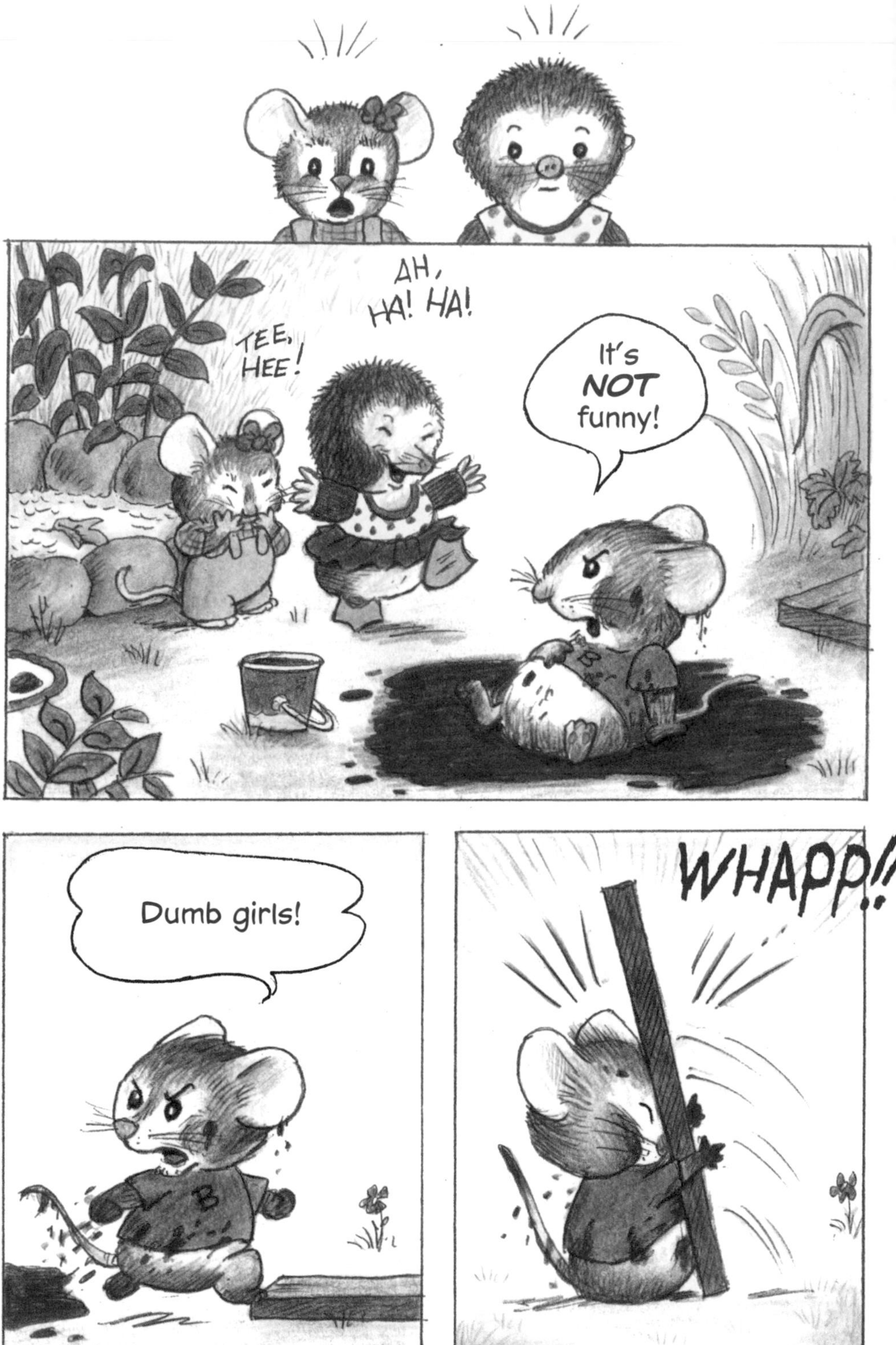
TEE, HEE!
AH, HA! HA!
It's **NOT** funny!
Dumb girls!
WHAPP!!

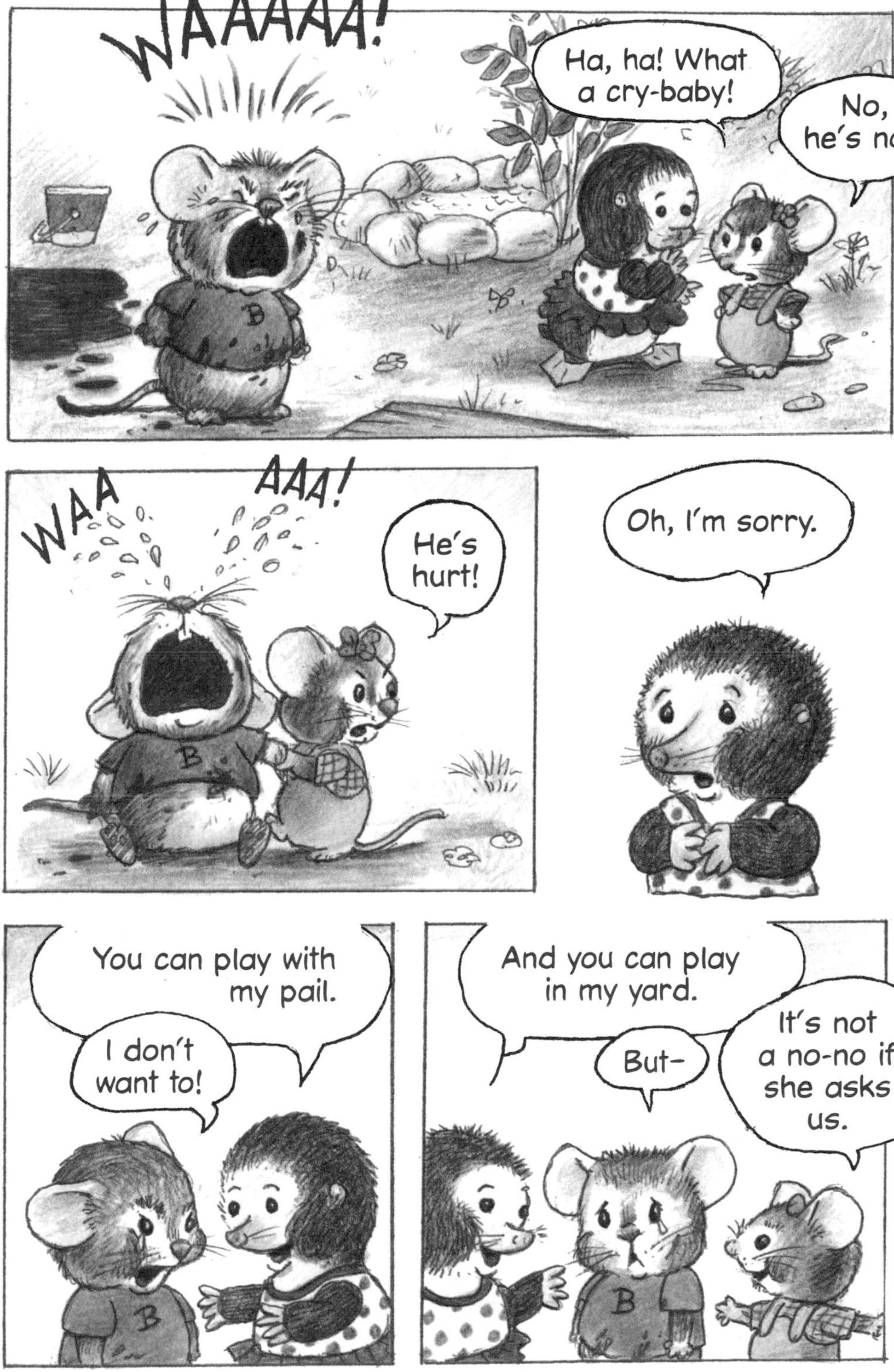
WAAAAA!
Ha, ha! What a cry-baby!
No, he's not!
WAA AAA!
He's hurt!
Oh, I'm sorry.
You can play with my pail.
I don't want to!
And you can play in my yard.
But-
It's not a no-no if she asks us.

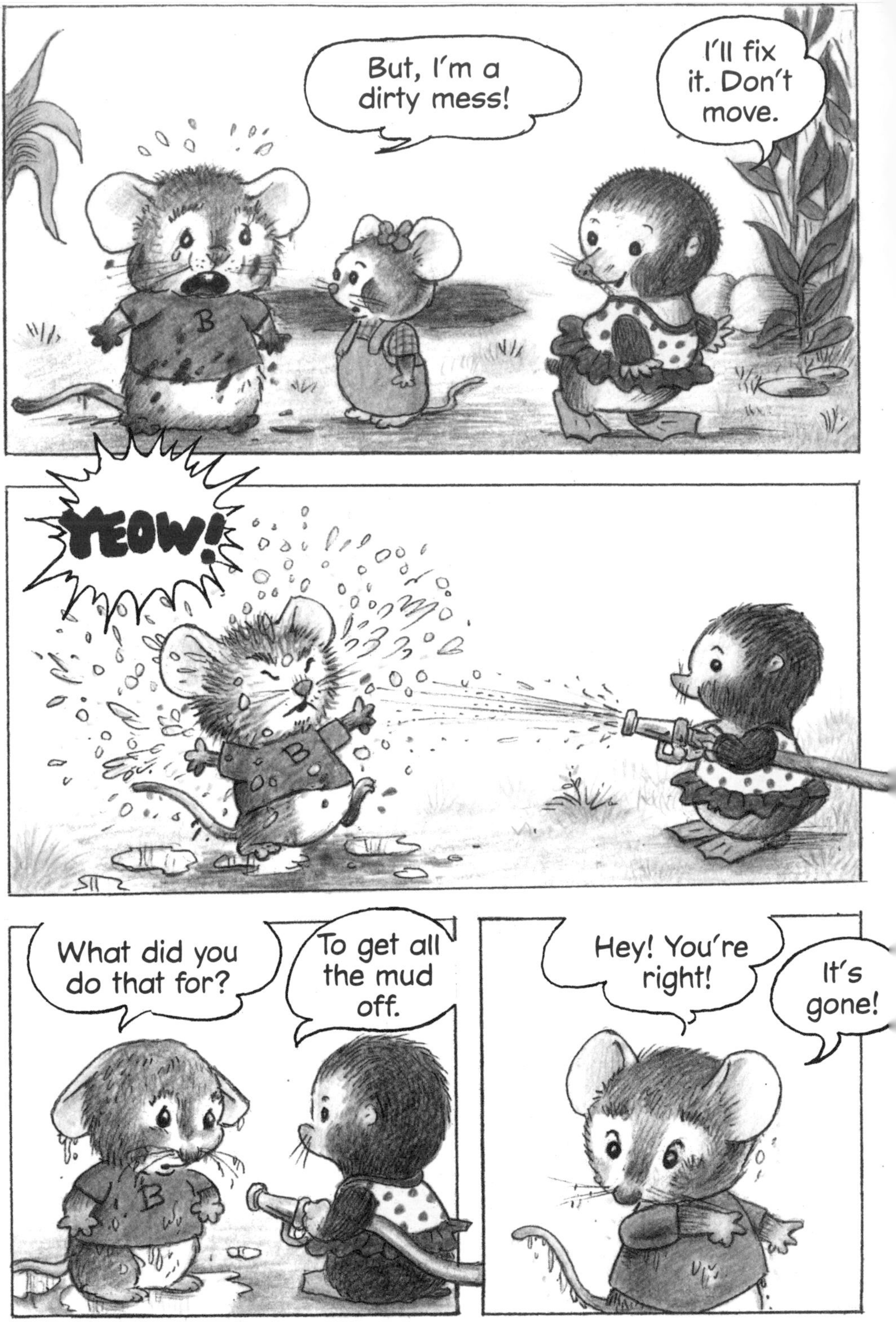
But, I'm a dirty mess!
I'll fix it. Don't move.
YEOW!
What did you do that for?
To get all the mud off.
Hey! You're right!
It's gone!

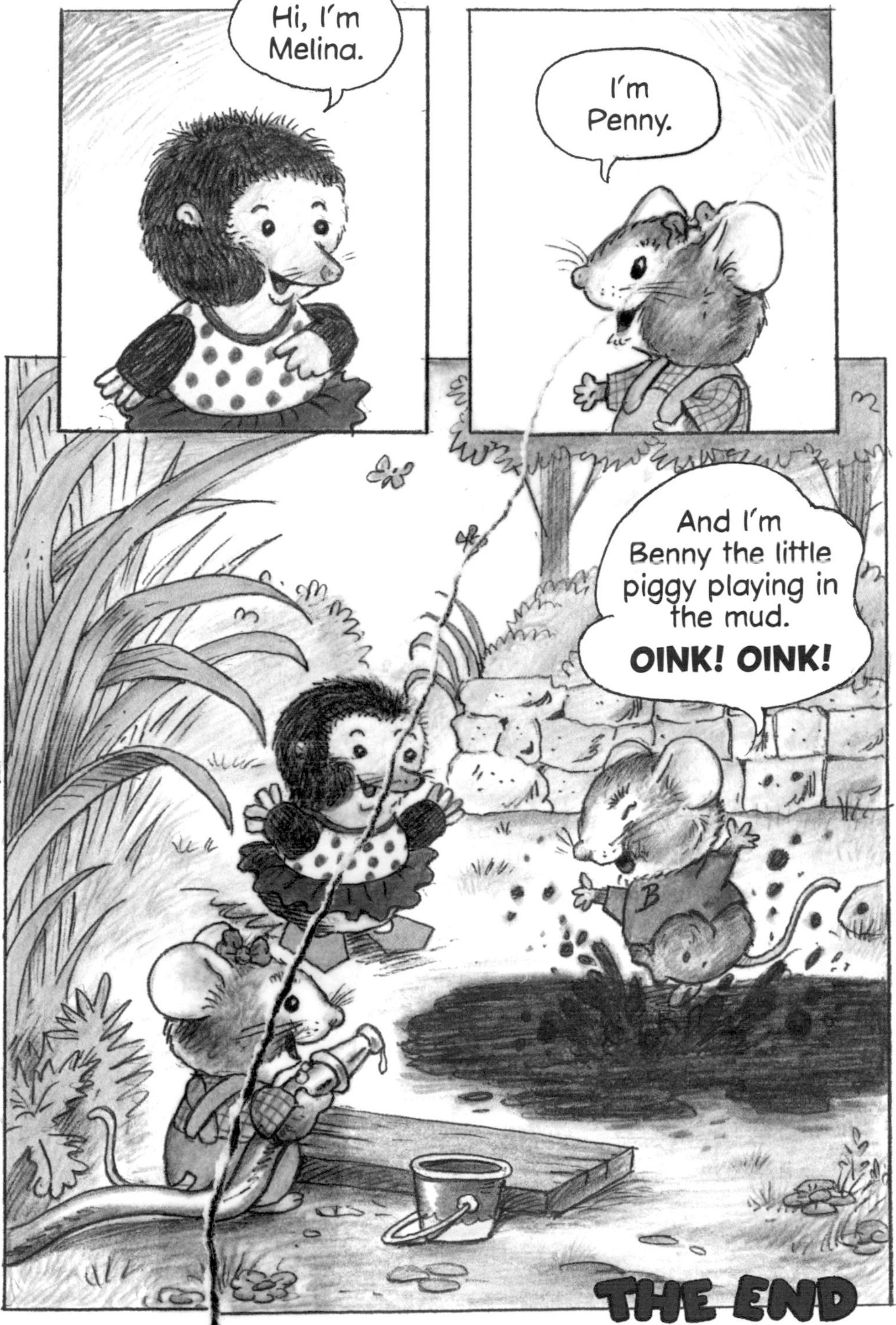
Hi, I'm Melina.
I'm Penny.
And I'm Benny the little piggy playing in the mud.
OINK! OINK!
THE END

# ABOUT THE AUTHOR

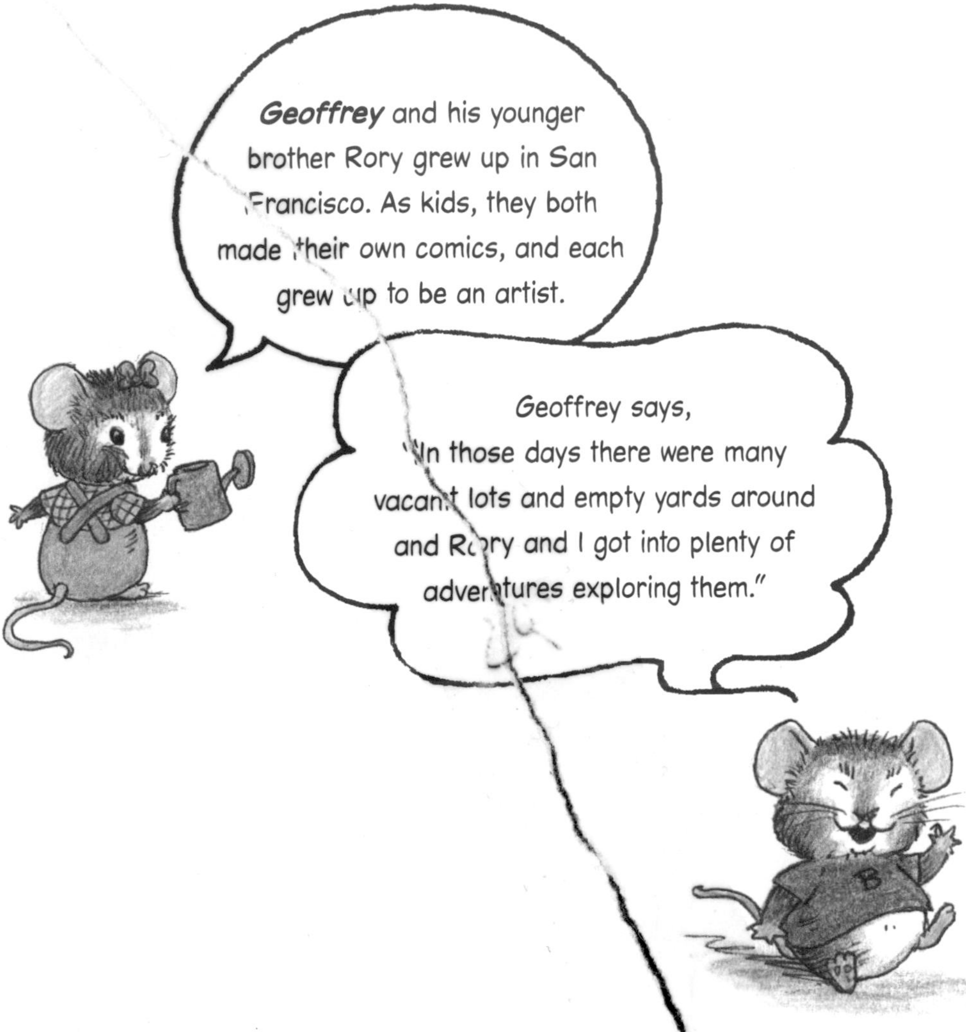
*Geoffrey* and his younger brother Rory grew up in San Francisco. As kids, they both made their own comics, and each grew up to be an artist.
Geoffrey says, "In those days there were many vacant lots and empty yards around and Rory and I got into plenty of adventures exploring them."

Geoffrey has written and illustrated over forty children's books, including the extremely popular series of early readers *Otto and Uncle Tooth*, the classic *Bear by Himself*, the *Patrick Bear* books, and *When the Wind Blew* by Caldecott Medal-winning author Margaret Wise Brown. His last TOON Book, *Benny and Penny in Just Pretend*, was praised in a *Booklist* starred review as "a charmer that will invite repeated readings."

# TOON INTO FUN at TOON-BOOKS.COM

**TOON READERS** are a revolutionary, free online tool that allows all readers to **TOON INTO READING!**

**TOON READERS**: you will love hearing the authors read their books when you click the balloons. TOON READERS are also offered in Spanish, French, Russian, Chinese and other languages, a breakthrough for all readers including English Language Learners.

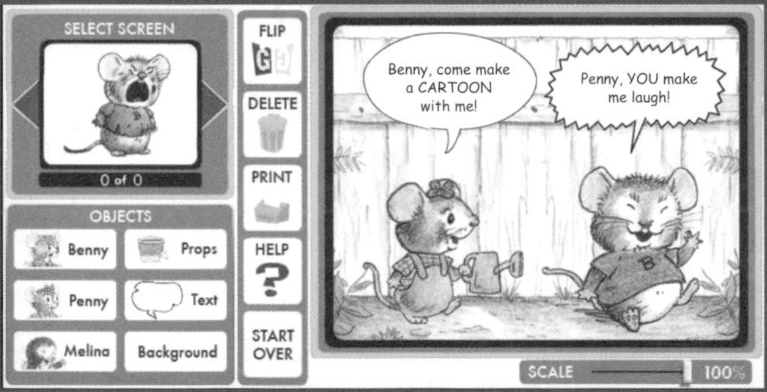
SELECT SCREEN
0 of 0
OBJECTS
Benny
Props
Penny
Text
Melina
Background
FLIP
DELETE
PRINT
HELP
START OVER
Benny, come make a CARTOON with me!
Penny, YOU make me laugh!
SCALE
100%

Young readers are young writers: our **CARTOON MAKER** lets you create your own cartoons with your favorite TOON characters.

Tune into our **KIDS' CARTOON GALLERY**: We post the funniest cartoons online for everyone to see. Send us your own and come read your friends' cartoons!

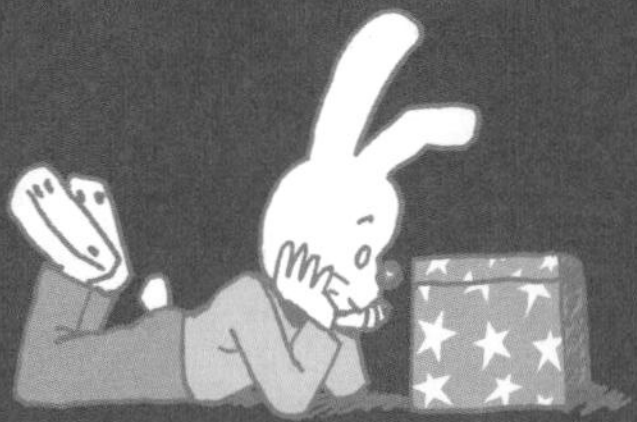

**Look for TOON Books on the iPhone!**